ON THIN ICE

BY KEVIN SYLVESTER

Scholastic Canada Ltd.
Toronto New York London Auckland Sydney
Mexico City New Delhi Hong Kong Buenos Aires

Dedicated to YOU!

Scholastic Canada Ltd.
604 King Street West, Toronto, Ontario M5V 1E1, Canada

Scholastic Inc.
557 Broadway, New York, NY 10012, USA

Scholastic Australia Pty Limited
PO Box 579, Gosford, NSW 2250, Australia

Scholastic New Zealand Limited
Private Bag 94407, Botany, Manukau 2163, New Zealand

Scholastic Children's Books
Euston House, 24 Eversholt Street, London NW1 1DB, UK

www.scholastic.ca

Library and Archives Canada Cataloguing in Publication
Title: On thin ice / Kevin Sylvester.
Names: Sylvester, Kevin, author, illustrator.
Description: Series statement: Hockey super six
Identifiers: Canadiana 20200236717 | ISBN 9781443163514 (softcover)
Classification: LCC PS8637.Y42 O5 2020 | DDC jC813/.6–dc23

6 5 4 3 2 1 Printed in Canada 139 20 21 22 23 24

STOP READING!

HIGH-PRIORITY SECURITY CLEARANCE REQUIRED

Place your eye as close as possible to the page for a retinal scan.

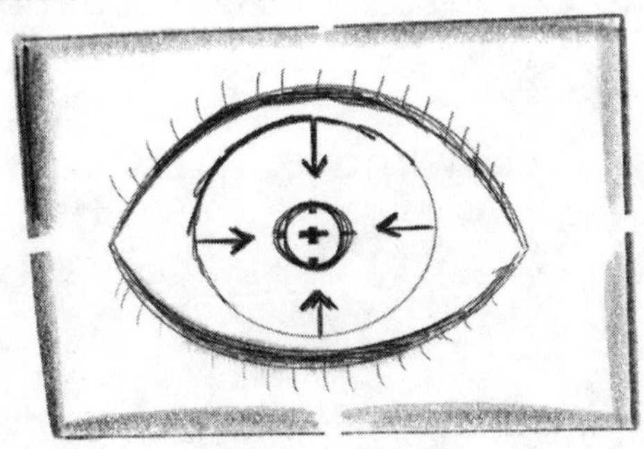

Confident you passed our security check?

GOOD! Now turn the page . . .

YOU DID PASS!

Whew! Good. We can call off the missile attack and you can keep reading.

These pages are the CONTINUING CASE FILES OF THE CHILDREN – MO, THE TWINS JENNY AND BENNY, DJ, STARLIGHT AND KARL – KNOWN AS THE HOCKEY SUPER SIX.

You may have been given security clearance to see the previously released top-secret files from HOCKEY SUPER SIX: THE PUCK DROPS HERE.

If so, you already know . . .

IN OUR PREVIOUS ADVENTURE

SIX HOCKEY-LOVING GEEKS WERE...

WHO ARE YOU CALLING A GEEK?

YEAH... THEY'RE GEEKS.

...ZAPPED BY A MYSTERIOUS FREEZE RAY...

...FIRED BY THIS DUDE, CLARENCE CROSSCHECK.

CROSSCHECK ORDERED A TEAM OF GIANT, ANGRY ICE SQUIDS TO ATTACK!

THE GEEKS DISCOVERED THEY NOW HAD HOCKEY SUPERPOWERS.
I'M SUPER STRONG!
I'M SUPER SMART!
WE'RE SUPER SYNCED!
I'M SUPER FAST!
I'M SUPER... NOT SURE?
M
J
B
D.J.
THEY DEFEATED THE ICE SQUIDS.
BUT... CROSSCHECK ESCAPED.
NOOOOOOOOOOOOOOO
NOW THE HOCKEY SUPER SIX AWAIT THE CALL... TO SAVE THE WORLD THROUGH HOCKEY!
6

If you were not given clearance to read that **TOP-SECRET DOSSIER** then you are hereby ordered to **FORGET EVERYTHING YOU HAVE JUST READ**.

If you refuse to forget what you have read, then . . . **BAD THINGS**.

WAS THAT A KNOCK AT YOUR DOOR?

If you do have clearance . . . well, you can ignore that masked commando on your roof and **TURN THE PAGE**.

CHAPTER ONE
WHERE WERE WE?

Oh yeah. At the end of the last mission, the Super Six had **JUST ACTIVATED THEIR NEW SUPER SUITS** – made for them by the secret global agency known as **GUMPP** (The Global Undisputed Menace and Peril Preparedness Council. The C is silent). **WHY HAD THEY ACTIVATED THE SUITS?** Because a pack of **GIANT LIZARDS** was about to **ATTACK** their **SCHOOL**, The Greater Ottawa–Outaouais Brainy (but not Brawny) Educational Regional School – **GOOBERS**, for short.

That's where they were now.

The Super Six blasted out of the school doors, **THE GROUND BELOW THEM FREEZING INTO A GIANT ICE PAD**.

DJ stopped in the middle of the door frame. "This looks just like a goal. If any dinos get past you, and I'm sure they will, I'll stop them from getting inside."

"LAST LINE OF DEFENCE," Karl said with a salute, skating past him.

"**SURE.**" DJ gave a theatrical yawn. He felt a certain satisfaction watching the other five set off to battle giant killer animals. For years he'd tried to warn people that monsters like these were lurking around every corner. People had laughed.

Well, who was laughing now? (FYI: he was.)

"I'll be here if needed," he called. Then he laughed. (See!)

Karl caught up to the others. The ice spread out ahead of them. **THE EYES OF THE BEASTS BLAZED RED.**

"**OOOHHH,**" Starlight said. "So mesmerizing."

THE LIZARDS LET OUT IMMENSE RASPING GROWLS and charged.

"That's not so mesmerizing," Starlight said.

Mo crunched his knuckles. "**BRING IT ON.**"

"I would suggest the double-trouble gambit," Karl said.

Karl was, by general agreement, the captain of the group. There was no evidence that he had, in fact, been given a superpower but he **WAS ALWAYS FULL OF IDEAS**.

"**DOUBLE-TROUBLE IT IS**," said the twins. Then they were off, **SKATING FASTER AND FASTER**, heading straight for the lead lizard, which gnashed its terrible teeth.

Jenny held out her stick. Benny didn't need her to say "grab hold." He just knew that's what he had to do. Benny grabbed the other end.

They skated beneath the creature's belly, narrowly avoiding its **RAZOR-SHARP TALONS**. The lizard crashed to the ice, **CRACKING IT WITH ITS WEIGHT.** It flailed its arms and legs, whining horribly as it tried and failed to stand on the slippery surface.

"**YOU BIG BABY**," Jenny and Benny said, in **PERFECT SYNC**. They did that a lot since getting zapped.

They stopped skating and admired their work. This was a mistake.

"**LOOK OUT!**" Mo yelled. But it was too late.

WHAM. Another lizard had snuck up behind them. It swung its tail, slapping the twins high into the air.

"**AHHHHHHHHHHHHHHHHHHHHH!**"

"I've got them!" Starlight called. She sped around at super speed, creating a whirlwind of snow with her sledge. It formed a giant pile in the middle of the ice. The twins fell onto it with a gentle **FTTTTTT**.

"Thanks!"

"No problem," Starlight said.

"**FOCUS!**" Karl called.

"Not a problem," Mo yelled.

He quickly neutralized the lizard that attacked the twins. “These two are ready for cleanup.”

Karl sighed. **CLEANUP WAS HIS ONE REAL JOB.** He pushed a button on his glove and a stream of hockey tape sprang from his skates. He sped around the fallen lizards, **WRAPPING THEM IN A TIGHT WEB OF TAPE**. They struggled, but stayed put.

“Nice work,” Starlight said.

“Work?” Karl looked around.

The twins were back up and using their **MIND POWERS TO CONFUSE YET ANOTHER LIZARD** by passing what looked like a lunchbox between its legs.

MO WAS USING HIS ENORMOUS STRENGTH TO TOPPLE ONE THAT HAD DARED TO ATTACK HIM. Starlight joined him and skated around the lizard so quickly it got dizzy and crashed to the ice.

They were doing super, exciting stuff. Karl didn't feel like he was doing much at all. Certainly nothing super.

"You can wrap this one up, captain," Mo said, pointing at his now prostrate prey.

The twins waved. "**COME OVER AND TIE UP THIS ONE TOO, CAPTAIN KARL!**"

"**TIE THIS ONE UP,**" Karl muttered under his breath. Was he really contributing anything?

Starlight was staring at a lizard, tapping her lips with her finger. Karl had seen that look before.

"**WHAT'S UP IN THAT SUPER BRAIN OF YOURS?**" he asked.

"As I suspected when we first spied these creatures, these are in fact super-sized geckos."

"Crosscheck," Karl said.

QUICK RECAP . . .

Crosscheck, you may recall, had used

a ray gun called a **SIZEMATRON 2000**. Karl's mom, the Prime Minister of Canada, had seized that weapon.

. . . END OF QUICK RECAP

Clearly Crosscheck, wherever he was now, had **ANOTHER ONE.**

Starlight shook her head sadly. "Geckos are usually a very gentle and good-natured lizard."

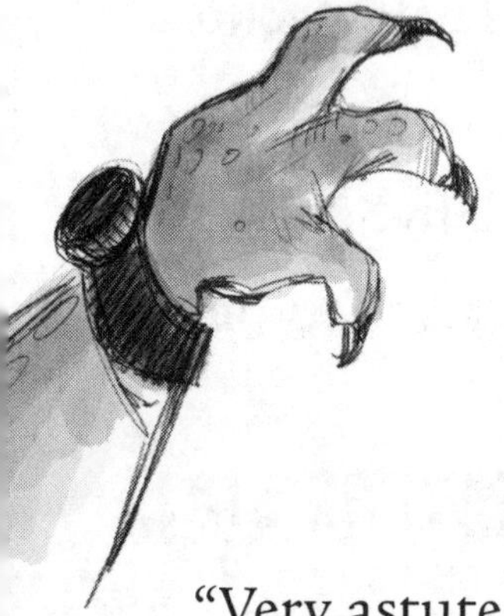

THE GECKO HISSED AND SPAT.

Karl pointed at a **PUCK-SHAPED WATCH-THINGY** wrapped around the wrist of the lizard. "**MIND CONTROL OF SOME KIND?**"

"Very astute observation," Starlight said.

She reached over and cracked the band.

The puck-watch **FELL TO THE ICE AND BEGAN FLASHING.**

"**OOOHHH,**" Starlight said, fascinated by the light. **IT BEGAN BEEPING.**

"**YIKES!**" Starlight slapped the watch into the nearby river. It **BLEW UP**, sending a spray of water into the air.

The gecko calmed down. In seconds it was gently snoring.

"The poor thing is worn out." Starlight stroked the cheek of the lizard. "Still a gentle gecko at heart."

"Well, whatever they are, we got all five of them," Karl said, taking in the field with a sweep of his hand.

Starlight gasped. "**BUT THERE WERE SIX!**"

CHAPTER TWO

DEEP-SIXED

DJ watched the battle with an amused smile. Forwards were so cute, the way they skated so hard on their tiny legs, wasting all that energy, getting tripped, knocked down, smacking into each other.

"**BEING A GOALIE IS THE BEST,**" he said.

"GRRRRRRR," said a voice above him.

"You said it . . . Mo?"

DJ looked out at the ice. All five of his friends were skating toward him. **INCLUDING MO.**

DJ looked up. **A GIANT GLOB** of slobber hit

him **IN THE HEAD.**

"I CAN'T SEE!"

Before he could wipe the slobber away, he was slammed hard onto the ice. Something heavy was on top of him, and it **BEGAN SQUEEZING HIS HELMET, TIGHTER AND TIGHTER**.

"It's not nice to crash a goalie's net," DJ said. The helmet began to crack. "**TIME FOR A PATENTED DJ SPIN-O-RAMA.**" In a flash he swung his legs around, turning like a top. The speed flung the slobber off his face, but not the giant gecko.

DJ kicked at its sides with his pads, **BUT THE BEAST HAD A HOLD ON HIM**. It stretched its neck back and opened its jaws, ready to strike.

"**THE WATCH!**" Starlight's voice pierced the air.

DJ spotted the lizard's wrist. "**LET'S SAVE THIS SITUATION!**" he chuckled. With a supersonic boom he flicked his titanium glove and **YANKED THE WRISTBAND OFF AND AWAY**.

The gecko instantly relaxed, its eyes drooping and rolling back in its head.

"**UH OH**," DJ said. He dug his skates into the ice and pushed himself backward and out from underneath the beast. The exhausted lizard fell down on the ice with a **WHUMP**, fast asleep.

DJ opened his glove and looked at the watch. **IT BEGAN TO BEEP.** He tossed it into the air. It

DISINTEGRATED IN A PUFF OF FLAME AND SMOKE.

"Nice work!" Starlight hugged DJ.

"Well, if any of you had bothered to backcheck I might have had a little help." He looked at Karl. "You wanna tie this one up too?"

Karl had a sudden urge to say, "**DO IT YOURSELF.**" But he skated over and taped the arms and legs of the beast together while the others high-fived and boasted about **HOW QUICKLY THEY'D BEEN ABLE TO STOP THE GECKOS AND SAVE THEIR SCHOOL.**

Karl sighed and pushed a button on his helmet. A face appeared on the inside of his visor.

"Yes, son?" It was his mom (and **SECRET HEAD OF GUMPP**), Prime Minister Pauline Patinage.

"**WE HAD A LITTLE INCIDENT,**" Karl said.

He swivelled his head so his mom could take in all the carnage. There were chunks of melting ice, a few gouges in the lawn of the school and a tree that a gecko, or possibly Mo, had knocked over.

"Tsk-tsk," PM PP said. "You should have called me."

"It happened really fast," Karl said. "And then we . . ." He paused. "**THEY TOOK CARE OF IT.** Can you send a cleanup crew to come and take these lizards to the zoo?"

"On it," PM Patinage said. **THERE WAS A BLIP AND HER FACE DISAPPEARED.**

"No 'Thanks, son'?" Karl huffily skated over to the group. "**WE SHOULD GO BACK UNDERCOVER FAST, BEFORE THE OTHER KIDS COME BACK.**"

"Aw!" Jenny and Benny said. "But we're having so much fun."

Karl pointed at the school doors. "**INSIDE NOW!**"

He shocked himself with how angry he sounded. But the others started sheepishly making their way back inside the cafeteria. "Yes, captain," they grumped.

Karl took a final look at the battlefield. All the other students had vanished, running away as far and as quickly as possible.

Good.

He turned around and skated inside the school.

AS HE DID, THE ICE MELTED.

CHAPTER THREE
THE GRASSY KNOW-IT-ALL

What Karl didn't see were two characters who had been **HIDING BEHIND** a hydrangea bush: Clarence Crosscheck, in disguise as the school's science teacher Mr. Gardien, and his robot sidekick Ron Dell, in disguise as his seriously weird-looking dog.

"I'm sorry, sir," Ron said, placing a paw on Crosscheck's shoulder.

Crosscheck began shaking, his body vibrating with spasms. Ron took his hand away. Crosscheck was unpredictable at the best of times, **AND THIS**

DIDN'T SEEM LIKE A GOOD TIME AT ALL.

Crosscheck started laughing, deeply and creepily. **RON PREPPED FOR ALMOST ANYTHING.** But Crosscheck calmed down, wiping tears from his eyes. "Oh Ron, Ron, Ron. **How SAD it is that LITTLE MINDS such as yours can only see the small picture.**"

Ron rolled his eye. "Oh, great genius. Do tell."

Crosscheck rubbed his hands together. "My plan is unfolding perfectly. Just as I have intended."

"YOU WANTED THE LIZARDS TO LOSE?"

"Obviously, you dolt, I would have preferred to see the lizards enjoy an after-school snack. But I anticipated that they would not be up to the combined forces of the six children.

Which means the children can be defeated in the NEXT STAGE of my plan."

"Next stage?"

Crosscheck **SMILED AN EVEN EVILER SMILE** than usual. "Yes. My robots."

Ron was about to ask **"WHAT ROBOTS?"** when the sound of approaching helicopters filled the air.

"Let us decamp to my lair," Crosscheck said. **"I've learned some interesting facts about the so-called Super Six. VERY INTERESTING INDEED."** With an **EVIL CACKLE**, he pressed a button on his watch, and he and Ron disappeared into a hole in the ground.

BUT LET'S NOT END THIS CHAPTER QUITE YET.

Because there were others who had been watching: **THE SIX NASTIEST KIDS AT THE SCHOOL, THE GANG** (short for Greatest Awesomest Nastiest GOOBERS). They had also been *filming*

from inside a dumpster in the parking lot.

"We can steal some of those sweet moves," Billy Crudbucket, the leader, said.

"The passing was pretty good," Gabby Gourd said.

"I WAS TALKING ABOUT THE TRIPPING AND SLASHING, YOU GOOF!" Billy said.

Frankie and JP, the **GANG** members, chuckled.

"But what's the deal with the short kid?" asked Lucretia Leather. "Is he the mascot or something?"

Billy replayed his video. "He didn't seem to do anything but clean up."

Gabby had an idea. "Hey! You think we could take him on?"

Lucretia sneered. **"YEAH. FOR SOME . . . PRACTICE."**

She made **THE WORD "PRACTICE" SOUND LIKE A THREAT**. She cracked her knuckles. That also sounded like a threat.

"Might be fun." Billy replayed the video. "If we can get him away from the others, I bet we could even steal that radical equipment." Billy pocketed the phone. "And I know a **CERTAIN SCIENCE TEACHER** who might be willing to exchange some free grades for a little intel."

Lucretia and Gabby looked confused. "Who?"

"Gardien, you blockheads!" Billy said.

He actually said a lot more, but the **ROARING OF THE HELICOPTERS** drowned it out.

CHAPTER FOUR
A STICKY SITUATION

Fast forward a few days, and Prime Minister Pauline Patinage had a lot on her plate. Literally. She'd just sat down at her desk to enjoy **A BREAKFAST OF PANCAKES AND MAPLE SYRUP** when a courier arrived with a wheelbarrow full of binders.

Without stopping to even say hello, he'd dumped the lot on top of the desk, turned, and marched away, **ALMOST ROBOTICALLY**.

Drips of maple syrup oozed from under the pile and **ONTO THE SHOCKED PM'S BEST SHOES**. The smiling face of her secretary, Mr. Filbert, appeared over the top of the pile.

"Good morning, PM PP," he said cheerily.

Patinage growled. **"CAN YOU PLEASE EXPLAIN THIS MESS?"**

"It's from the Leader of the Opposition."

"Bu—"

PAUSE.

Okay, without getting too deeply into the inner workings of the Canadian parliamentary system, the bottom line is that PM PP was leader of the ruling party. They got the most MPs (Members of Parliament) elected in the last election, so they make up the government.

The party that finishes in second place in an election is called the Opposition. Their main job is to **YELL AT THE RULING PARTY** for at least an hour every day in something called Question Period. It's called that because . . . why do they set aside an hour every day for politicians to yell at each other? **GOOD QUESTION.**

A week before, something strange had happened with the Opposition. They showed up for work looking slightly . . . different. Shiny. **THEY SQUEAKED WHEN THEY WALKED.** And they hardly yelled at all anymore. They mostly sat staring straight ahead. And they'd elected a new leader, Rob Ott, who **SPOKE IN A BORING MONOTONE.**

And they didn't seem to sleep. PM PP had walked by their offices and heard the **NON-STOP CLICKETY-CLACK** of fingers on keyboards.

She was about to discover what they had been working on . . .

UNPAUSE

"—t."

"It's a new **HOCKEY GAME LAW**," Filbert said, reading the gold print on the cover.

"HOCKEY GAME?"

Filbert opened the binder. "The subtitle is ominous. It says: A law pertaining to **THE TRANSFER OF POWER FOLLOWING THE**

SUCCESSFUL COMPLETION OF A HOCKEY GAME between the controlling powers of . . . It actually goes on for a while."

"Sounds like Ott. I can hear his voice." **THEN SHE SAT BOLT UPRIGHT.** "Wait. Did you say this is **ACTUALLY A LAW?**"

Filbert nodded.

"But . . . but how did that happen? Only the government can make a new law."

"Remember last week when the Opposition was allowed to read out the details of their economic plan?"

She remembered. Ott had gone on for so long, in such a droning voice, **THAT EVERYONE HAD FALLEN ASLEEP. WAIT . . . NOT EVERYONE.**

"Those sneaks!" PM PP said. "**THEY VOTED ON THIS WHILE THE REST OF US WERE OUT COLD!**"

"It would appear so. Oh . . . OH," Filbert said, **HIS EYES GROWING WIDE.**

"What?"

He pointed to a line in sub-paragraph 23b of Appendix ZZZZZZZZZZZ.

PM PP LOOKED AND GASPED.

Filbert's voice shook. "It says that if the Opposition's team wins the game, they **SEIZE CONTROL OF THE GOVERNMENT!**" He chewed his fingernail. "And the **GAME IS SCHEDULED FOR TOMORROW** on Parliament Hill!"

Filbert threw a hand in front of his forehead. "I feel faint."

PM Patinage, on the other hand, was completely calm as she settled back in her chair. "Relax, Filbert. It's all going to be okay. **I HAVE A PLAN**."

CHAPTER FIVE
HATCHED

Ron pulled a fresh batch of cookies out of the oven. **THEY SMELLED WONDERFUL.** He couldn't really eat them, but he enjoyed making them. He would sneak the treats to the various zoo captives that his boss had locked up **INSIDE THE DEEPEST DEPTHS OF THE LAIR.** So far he hadn't been caught.

"Perhaps the marauding marmots would like some . . ." He stopped as the double doors of the kitchen hissed open. Ron quickly hid the cookie sheet behind his back.

Crosscheck walked in. **"What is that HORRIBLE stench?"** He pretended to throw up.

Ron narrowed his eye. Some day his "boss" was going to push him too far.

Crosscheck waved his hands to clear the air. "It doesn't matter. **Where's my FISH BRAIN SMOOTHIE?"**

Ron slipped the cookies into his butt – well, a secret compartment in his backside anyway – and walked over to the fridge. He pulled out a glass filled with a thick grey concoction and handed it to Crosscheck.

The evil scientist took a long gulp and let out a contented sigh. In truth it tasted like eating farts, but Crosscheck was convinced it made him smarter.

"So, you're probably wondering about my new plan."

Ron wasn't, actually, but knew it didn't matter.

"I've examined **THE GANG's video a hundred times** and it confirms what I suspected"

"And that is?"

"They can be split up and defeated."

Crosscheck began tapping his fingers together excitedly. "If my theory is right, and . . ." He looked at Ron.

Fine, Ron thought, *I'll bite*. "And they always are . . ."

"The TINY ONE is the key."

Ron scratched his head. "BUT HE'S **THE WEAKEST.**"

Crosscheck lowered his head and looked at Ron like he was a little child. **"AU CONTRAIRE."**

Ron was skeptical. "IF YOU **SAY SO.**"

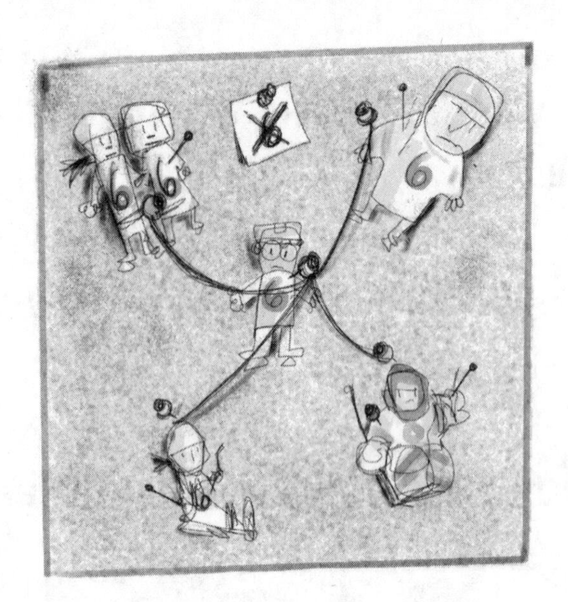

"I do. Which means you do too."

"FINE. SO, WHAT DO WE DO NOW?" Ron asked.

"WE KIDNAP HIM."

"What?" Ron was worried he'd asked one too many questions.

"The wheels are in MOTION." As if on cue, there was a loud ring on Crosscheck's watch. He answered it and leaned back farther in his chair.

"Ah, BILLY CRUDBUCKET. Just the person I wanted to speak to."

CHAPTER SIX
MATCHED

Karl walked down the school hallway, a stack of books precariously balanced in the crook of his arm. He was thinking. *How do I become Super?*

He didn't see **BILLY AND THE GANG UNTIL IT WAS TOO LATE**. They were huddled against the lockers, watching Billy's phone, when Karl bumped into them. **OOF!** Billy's phone and Karl's books went flying.

"Hey, nerd!" Gabby said grabbing him by the collar. "Pick that up!"

KARL GRITTED HIS TEETH. If only he were as strong as Mo, or as obnoxious as DJ.

But he wasn't.

He leaned down and reached for the phone. Billy's video was still playing. It was a close-up of him in disguise, **TAPING UP A GECKO** while the other five were **HEROICALLY BATTLING THE LIZARDS**.

Billy's voice could be heard clearly over the battle: **"WHAT'S THIS DOPE'S SUPERHERO NAME, THE JANITOR? HA, HA, HA."**

Then Gabby's voice. "It's like he's the mascot. Ha, ha, ha."

Karl's cheeks burned. *Don't blow your cover.* He lifted the phone and handed it to Billy.

Billy smirked. **"THAT RUNT IS A WORSE HOCKEY PLAYER THAN YOU!"**

Karl growled.

"WHAT? YOU WANNA DEFEND THAT LOSER?" Billy said, waving the phone in Karl's face.

The other **GANG** members laughed derisively.

"He's not a loser," Karl said.

Billy snorted. "Seriously? Watch the video again."

KARL'S FINGER HOVERED OVER HIS SECRET BUTTON. He could teach these bullies a lesson. **ALL HE HAD TO DO WAS . . .**

There was a cough from their left. **"Is there a problem?"** It was Mr. Gardien – who of course was really Crosscheck – standing in the doorway to the lab.

"No problem, Mr. Gardien," Billy said. "I was just showing this doofus **HOW USELESS THAT KID WITH THE C WAS DURING THAT FIGHT**."

Gardien reached for the phone. He watched

it, **SEEMINGLY AMUSED**. (Of course he'd seen it a **HUNDRED TIMES ALREADY**.)

"Yes. **My INCREDIBLE scientific brain** can easily see the qualitative difference between **THIS CHILD and the other TRULY HEROIC PLAYERS**."

"Yeah," said Billy. "He's a loser. Ha, ha, ha."

Karl clenched his fists. He glared at Billy.

WEIRDLY, GARDIEN WAS NOW GLARING AT BILLY TOO.

Billy kept chuckling.

Gardien coughed. "Is that **ALL** you have to say, Billy?"

"Um. Yeah? Isn't it?"

Gardien's dog chomped Billy's leg.

"OW!" But it seemed to shake something in Billy's brain. "Oh. Yes. I was wondering if there was a way to . . ." He lost his train of thought.

Gardien rubbed his forehead with his fingers. **"Why not CHALLENGE this pretender TO A HOCKEY GAME, you say?"**

Billy nodded furiously. "Yeah. That's what I said. Yeah. **IF ONLY THERE WAS A WAY TO CHALLENGE THIS PHONY HOCKEY PLAYER TO A REAL GAME.**"

Mr. Gardien shook his head. "*Tsk-tsk.* If only we knew a way to send him a message. Like, 'show up at **GOOBERS ARENA** tonight at seven, and prove that you know how to play this game.' Isn't that what you meant Billy?"

Billy blinked.

"RIGHT, BILLY?"

Billy nodded. "**YEAH. SEVEN PM. TONIGHT. GOOBERS ARENA.**"

"What a good idea, Billy!" Gardien said. "But, alas, we have no idea how to do that. So the message, 'meet me tonight at seven pm at **GOOBERS ARENA**' will never be delivered. Sigh. Well, back to class everyone." Gardien shooed them away. Ron barked.

GARDIEN GRINNED AN EVIL GRIN.

But Karl didn't see it as he walked away with a smile on his own face. "**I'LL SHOW THEM WHO'S A LOSER.**"

CHAPTER SEVEN
SQUIRRELLY

C'mon Karl. **WE'RE A TEAM!**" Mo wrapped his arms around Karl and gave him a giant bear hug.

"Yeah, buddy," the twins said. **"YOU'RE THE CAPTAIN!"**

"Your mom has called a practice for tonight at seven," Starlight said. "**THERE'S A 100 PERCENT CHANCE THAT IT'S IMPORTANT.**"

Mo nodded. "She said Mr. Filbert, her assistant, would be there to coach."

Karl waved his hand in the air. "I've got a . . .

well, a something I can't miss. **YOU FIVE ARE THE REAL . . .**

"**OUCH!**" Karl flinched as DJ pinched his arm. "What was that for?"

"You sound like a demented squirrel **DRESSED** as Karl."

"Goalies!" Karl said, rubbing his arm. "I'm Karl, you bonehead."

DJ glared at him. "**THE KARL I KNOW WOULDN'T SKIP A PRACTICE FOR ANYTHING.**" He fished an acorn out of a pocket and held it up. "Hungry?"

"For crying out loud," Karl said. "I just have a thing I can't get out of. Not that you need me . . ." he added.

Mo cocked his head. "Is this what that's about?"

Starlight wheeled closer. "Karl. **WE'RE A TEAM.** Even if you don't have an . . . **EVIDENT** superpower."

EVIDENT. Karl took a deep breath. "Maybe . . .

Maybe I **DO** have a superpower – **BUT YOU FIVE ARE HOLDING ME BACK?**"

Starlight looked skeptical. "Hmmm . . . there's no evidence . . ."

Karl hurried on. "**MAYBE IF I TRY SOMETHING ON MY OWN, LIKE A SOLO GAME . . .**" He stopped himself from revealing any details about his rendezvous. **IT WOULD BE JUST LIKE THEM TO COME SAVE "POOR WEAK KARL" FROM HIMSELF.**

NO. HE WAS GOING. ALONE.

"It doesn't matter. I'll join you later. Maybe. Have fun."

He marched away.

"Poor deluded squirrel," DJ said, shaking his head sadly.

TALES FROM THE RINK

10¢

FEATURING

THE GANG

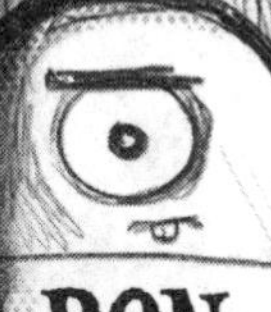

RON

ROBOTS

FEAR

OUTSIDE THE GOOBERS' RINK.

KARL FELT A PANG OF GUILT. IF HE TURNED AROUND HE COULD STILL MAKE PRACTICE. THEN...

HAHAHAHAHAHAHAHAHA

THERE WAS LAUGHTER. NOT THE GOOD KIND. THIS WAS THE KIND YOU'D HEAR FROM SOMEONE WHO'S JUST PULLED UP ANOTHER KID'S UNDERWEAR.

THE GANG. THEY WERE INSIDE, **LAUGHING** AT HIM.

SHOWTIME!

KARL PUSHED THE **K** ON HIS TIEPIN AND TRANSFORMED INTO **CAPTAIN KARL.**

HAHAHAHAHAHAHAHAHAHAHAHAHAHA
HE RUSHED THROUGH THE DOORS AND STOPPED. ALL THE LIGHTS WERE OFF.
AN EERIE BLUE LIGHT SHIMMERED ACROSS THE RINK. THE EMPTY RINK.
KARL HAD NO TIME TO FLEE. THERE WAS A LOUD...
SNAP
AND THE WHOLE WORLD WENT DARK.

CHAPTER NINE
POWER PLAY

The sun peeked through the clouds in thin strips. A giant artificial rink shimmered in the light.

The temporary **BLEACHERS WERE PACKED** for what the national newspaper, the *Goat and Quail*, had dubbed the **"PARLIAMENTARY PASSING OF POWER" HOCKEY GAME**.

Of course PM PP's plan was to have her squad of six super kids battle the Opposition Team and win. There was **JUST ONE HITCH**. Only five had shown up.

"Where's Karl?" PM PP asked.

"Isn't he with you?"

PM PP shook her head. "He texted me last night that he was going to sleep in. He must have been exhausted from practising with you five."

Mo looked totally shocked. "**HE NEVER SHOWED UP.**"

PM PP furrowed her eyebrows. "But he sent me a picture of himself AT practice." She held up her phone.

Starlight looked at it closely. "**THIS IS A FAKE,**" she said. "The angle of reflected light off his helmet is inconsistent with the angle of the overhead lighting."

"Yeah. **AND HE'S WEARING A BATHING SUIT.**" Mo pointed at the phone.

"Yes. That too," said Starlight.

"What are we going to do?" PM PP said. "**WHERE'S MY SON!?!?**"

Her phone buzzed. It was a text: an image of Karl dressed in his equipment, saying, "on my way."

PM PP relaxed a bit. "He's going to have some explaining to do when he does get here. But we need to win this game, with or without him."

THE SUPER SIX MINUS ONE NODDED.

The PM continued, "I didn't tell you this yet, but the first thing Rob Ott says he will do is **TURN ALL THE SCHOOLS INTO WORKSHOPS**."

"Isn't that illegal?" Starlight said.

"Now, yes. But if we lose this game, there's no telling what could happen. **THE FUTURE OF OUR VERY NATION IS DEPENDING ON YOU**."

"Easy peasy, PM," said the twins. "Now who are we going to humiliate?" They scanned the horizon for the other team and their wayward captain.

Finally a referee skated to centre ice, her arms moving back and forth in strict precision, and a slight metallic squeaking coming from her knees.

Her voice, even without a microphone, boomed: **"TODAY. WE. WILL. PLAY. A. HOCKEY. GAME. THE GOVERNMENT. IS. REPRESENTED BY. FIVE . . . CHILDREN. HA. HA. HA."**

The crowd laughed too. **FIVE KIDS? WHAT CHANCE COULD THEY HAVE?**

Still no Karl.

Mo nodded at Starlight, his defence partner. "I guess we'll have to do this short-handed."

"I calculate that **OUR CHANCES ARE STILL 99.999999999 PERCENT IN FAVOUR OF WINNING**, depending on variables."

"Variables?" DJ asked.

Before Starlight could elaborate, the ref's voice boomed out again: **"NOW. MEET. THE. OPPOSITION. TEAM."**

The five children gasped as **SIX ENORMOUS ROBOTS MADE THEIR WAY TOWARD THE RINK.** They stood as **HIGH AS THREE MOS**. Instead of skates, they moved on treads, like tanks, which whirred and whined. **THEIR EYES GLOWED AN EERIE RED.**

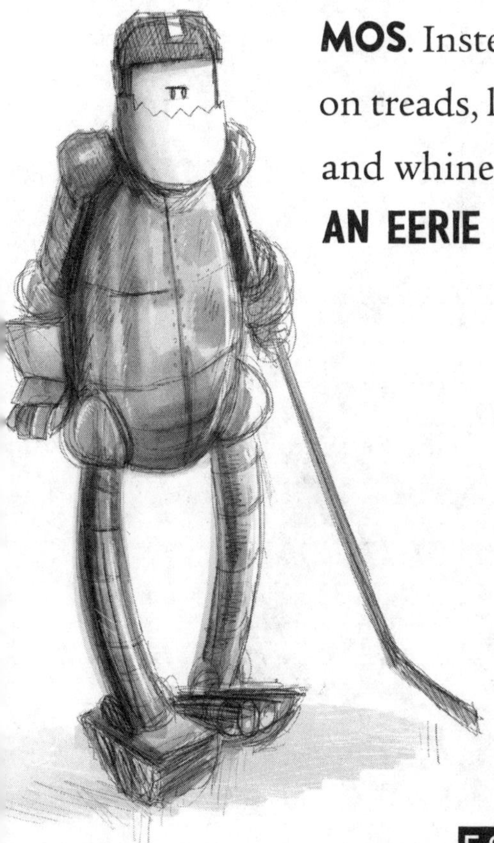

"Are those variables?" DJ called, pointing at the robots.

Starlight nodded. "**PROBABILITY NOW 98.534 PERCENT.**"

The crowd buzzed with excitement.

The ref continued, **"FIRST. TEAM. TO. SCORE. SEVEN. GOALS. WINS."**

Mo cracked his knuckles.

The twins tapped their sticks.

DJ slapped the goalposts with his stick. **"LET'S SEE IF WE CAN BETTER THE ODDS."**

The ref blew the whistle and dropped the puck.

CHAPTER TEN
KING KARL

Karl awoke to the smell of cookies. He blinked. A **GIANT ONE-EYED HOCKEY PUCK** was holding out a **PLATE OF WARM, GOOEY GOODNESS**. He looked weirdly familiar, but Karl couldn't quite place him.

"You must be hungry," the puck said.

IT TALKED? WHY WAS THAT FAMILIAR TOO?

WHERE WAS HE? Carved rock walls rose from the floor. **A CAVE OF SOME KIND.** Through a doorway he could see a room filled with test tubes, computers and blinking lights. **A LAB?**

Karl pushed himself upright in his chair. His hands almost sank into the fabric.

"**WHOA. SO SOFT.**" He was **SITTING ON A THRONE** of plush red velvet and deep rich oak.

The puck pointed behind his head. Karl turned and saw **A LARGE GOLD CROWN WITH A K** emblazoned underneath.

The puck pointed at Karl's body. He was wearing a bathrobe **WITH HIS FACE ON IT.** He looked down at his feet. His slippers had his own face on them.

His lips began to tremble. "**NOW THIS IS THE KIND OF TREATMENT I'VE ALWAYS FELT I DESERVE.**"

Ron smiled. "Yes. My boss believes **YOU ARE THE MOST IMPORTANT OF THE . . . SUPER SIX.**"

Karl gulped. "Super what?"

"WE KNOW WHO YOU REALLY ARE, KARL PATINAGE."

"WE? YOUR BOSS?"

Ron jammed a cookie into Karl's mouth.

"Wait," Karl said. "First off, this is delicious."

Ron blushed. "Why, thank you."

"And second, **WHY AM I NOT AT THE HOCKEY RINK? WHERE'S THE GANG?"**

Ron held up Karl's cellphone.

Carl. Sorry . . . had to have government
agents prevent you from revealing your
identity to the GANG.Yes, Mole and the
others told me what you were up to.
This is four the best.
Let my friends pamper you. Soon your true
power will be revealed to the world!
PM PP

"**PM PP? SEEMS KIND OF FORMAL,**" Karl said. "**AND WHY DID SHE SPELL MY NAME WITH A C? AND DID SHE MEAN MO?**"

Ron coughed. "I'm sure it was just a slip of the thumb." **HE SNATCHED THE PHONE BACK.**

"Hey!"

"It needs to be plugged in." He hurriedly offered Karl another cookie.

Karl munched it down with a contented sigh. "What did she mean about my power? **I DON'T HAVE A POWER.**"

Ron smiled. "My boss and I observed something **VERY INTERESTING** as you and the team battled the lizards that some, um, **EVIL TYPE PERSON WHO'S NOT AT ALL LIKE MY BOSS** sent to destroy the city."

Karl's shoulders sagged. The puck, he was certain, was about to burst his bubble by pointing out how useless he'd been. "Look, I can explain . . ."

"No need. The other five are clearly nothing without you," said Ron.

Karl's mouth froze open.

"YOU ARE THE CHOSEN ONE."

Karl closed his mouth slowly and settled back in his chair. "Tell me more . . . about myself."

It was as his boss had predicted. *The boy will fall sway to flattery*. Ron felt an unexpected twinge of sadness. "Well. Without your **CHARM, INTELLIGENCE, AND MASTERFUL TAPING TECHNIQUE**, the city would be in ruins."

"Go on." Karl grabbed a handful of cookies and let it all wash over him.

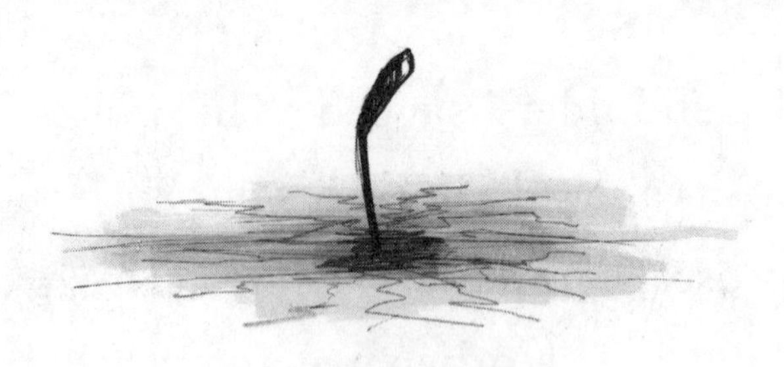

CHAPTER ELEVEN

UH-OH

The puck hit the ice with a slap. So did the first robot. **AS SOON AS IT TRIED TO MOVE SIDEWAYS ON THE ICE IT SLIPPED AND FELL.**

The twins smiled as they passed the puck back and forth between the legs of another. It also tumbled as it tried to swivel and pivot to follow the speedy kids.

JENNY SLAMMED THE PUCK INTO THE NET FOR A QUICK 1-0 LEAD.

"**WHOO-HOO!**" she yelled.

"**HOO-WHOO,**" Benny yelled, slightly behind Jenny.

They stopped and stared at each other. They'd been so in sync lately.

"**WEIRD,**" Jenny said.

"**ODD,**" Benny said, **NOT AT THE SAME TIME**.

The ref's whistle snapped their attention back to centre ice. They barely noticed the **SLIGHTLY SLOSHY NOISE THEIR SKATES MADE** as they took their places at the faceoff.

The puck dropped. This time Benny got it and raced on net. **ANOTHER SHOT, ANOTHER GOAL: 2-0.**

"Whoop!" he yelled, skating back for another faceoff.

"Hey," Jenny yelled back. "**I WAS WIDE OPEN**. Why didn't you pass to me?"

"You already have a goal," Benny said. "You want the puck? Try and get it off me." **HE DUG IN HIS SKATES TO SPRAY HER WITH SNOW.** Instead he slipped, splashing her with **A WAVE OF SLUSH**.

Jenny's mouth hung open. "You. You . . . JERK!"

She raced at her brother, who skated away, sending up a rooster tail of **EVEN MORE SLUSH**.

Starlight had seen the twins act like this before, but not since they'd been transformed into the **SUPER SIX**. *This bears some further observation*, she thought.

But before she could make any mental notes, the ref dropped the puck. **WITH NO TWINS THERE TO GRAB IT, THE PUCK TRICKLED OVER TO A PRONE ROBOT.**

With a loud crack, the robot whipped at the puck with a stick and sent it flying toward DJ.

He caught it easily. “That all you got?” DJ dropped the puck onto the ice. **HE DIDN'T NOTICE THE SPLASH AS IT LANDED IN A PUDDLE.**

Starlight noticed, but wasn’t sure what to make of it . . . yet.

Up in the government’s seats, PM PP breathed a sigh of relief. “At this rate we should wrap up this game easily.”

Her phone buzzed. A text from Karl:

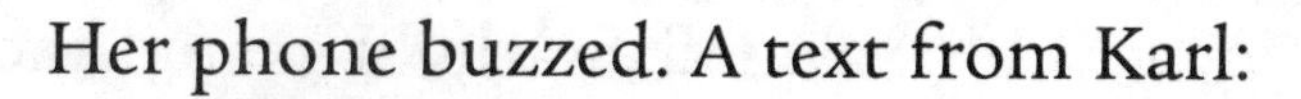

Be there soon. Karl (with a K) Patinage.

"KARL PATINAGE? SEEMS KIND OF FORMAL."

She was about to reply when a cheer from the crowd turned her attention back to the game.

MO HAD SCORED ON A SLAP SHOT FROM BEHIND HIS OWN NET.

Photographers from every paper in the land snapped pictures of the celebrating kids and the flailing robots.

"IT'S A ROUT!" A nearby government MP called out, a huge smile on her face.

Within just seconds, the **SUPER SIX** minus one were up 5–0 and **ON THEIR WAY TO AN EASY VICTORY**.

Mo yawned. Starlight skated back to chat with DJ, who looked like he might be asleep. **THE ROBOTS KEPT**

FALLING and seemed to take forever to get back up. They had barely touched the puck, let alone taken a second shot on net.

"**WHAT KIND OF USELESS HOCKEY TEAM IS THIS?**" PM PP smiled from the stands. She looked over at the Opposition MPs. They were seated together, their heads swivelling back and forth in **ALMOST PERFECT UNISON** as they followed the play.

They aren't wearing winter coats? she thought. **IT'S FEBRUARY! IN CANADA!**

She spotted Ott, expecting a frown, or maybe a single tear running down his cheek as **HIS MASTER PLAN FOR SEIZING POWER CRUMBLED IN FRONT OF HIS VERY EYES**. But as he spotted the PM looking at him, the sides of his mouth twisted into something resembling a doll's smile. **IT GAVE HER THE CREEPS.**

"What the heck . . ." Patinage started to say. Then another sound came from the crowd. **NOT A CHEER, BUT A HUGE GROAN.**

PM PP looked down at the ice and **COULDN'T BELIEVE HER EYES**.

CHAPTER TWELVE
ALL WET

"WHAT IS GOING ON?" Jenny shouted. Benny, right behind her, was **TOO SHOCKED TO ANSWER**.

Just **SECONDS BEFORE** they had been **RUSHING AROUND A ROBOT**. Jenny had stolen the puck and was swooshing toward the net to score a sixth goal. Benny was chasing her. **THEY'D SKATED FASTER AND FASTER. THEN . . . THEY'D LURCHED TO A STOP.**

Jenny looked down. Not only had she stopped, but **SHE WAS IN A DEEP, WET HOLE, HER KNEES**

TRAPPED IN STICKY, SUCKY MUD. She tried to lift her leg but it only made the mud grip her more tightly.

"**WHAT THE . . . ?**"

BENNY WAS JUST AS STUCK. He looked back. Like the trail from an airplane, there was a line of **COMPLETELY MELTED ICE** that stretched out behind each of them.

Starlight skated as close to them as she dared. "**SOMETHING IS WRONG,**" she said.

"Duh. Do ya think?" Benny asked, not hiding his annoyance. "**YOU'RE SUPPOSED TO BE THE BRAINIAC.**"

"Yeah, what happened" Jenny added.

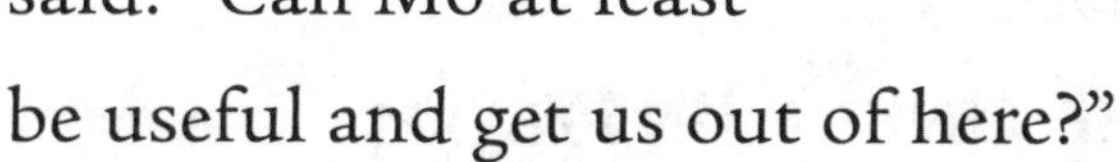

Starlight thought for a moment. "**I NEED MORE DATA.**"

"Oh for crying out loud," Benny said. "Can Mo at least be useful and get us out of here?"

They looked over at Mo, who was skating toward them at top speed. In a flash, **HE TOO FELL THROUGH A CRACK IN THE ICE AND DISAPPEARED.**

"**THIS HAS NEVER HAPPENED BEFORE,**" Starlight said, tapping her chin. "**WHY NOW?**"

The sky was cloudy. Her breath froze in the cool air. **WERE THE ROBOTS SHOOTING SOME KIND OF HEAT RAY, TO MELT THE ICE?**

"But there's no evidence of that, at all," she said out loud.

"**I BET IT'S THERMAL MICE,**" DJ called from the net. "Digging tunnels under the ice. Look out!"

A **ROBOT HAD GRABBED THE PUCK** and was now **MOVING CAUTIOUSLY FORWARD**. The other four joined it in a line. Large cracks began to appear in the ice.

"**STOP! THE RINK IS UNSTABLE!**" Starlight called out.

The robots ignored her warning and marched toward DJ. In seconds, **THEIR WEIGHT BROKE THROUGH THE ICE**. It shattered, a shard sending Starlight hurtling.

BUT THE ROBOTS WEREN'T TRAPPED. Their treads churned, throwing mud and ice chunks onto the rink as they rose over the sides of their craters and out.

Starlight realized that **THE ROBOTS HAD EXPECTED THIS.** They were built for these conditions. **BUT WHY HAD THE ICE FAILED?**

A robot took a shot from just a few metres from the goal. DJ stood his ground but the blast was so hard it blew him back and into the net.

The ref blew her whistle: **"GOAL!"** 5-1.

DJ shot the puck out disgustedly and skated back into his crease. Then, one of the robots

SWUNG ITS STICK AND TOOK OUT HIS LEGS.

DJ flew around in an almost complete circle and landed on his butt.

"**HEY! REF. THAT'S A PENALTY!**" he called.

But **THE REF JUST SKATED AWAY** and got ready to drop the puck back at centre ice.

"Ref. I said, **THAT'S A PENALTY!**" DJ yelled.

She blew her whistle. **"GOALIE. TWO. MINUTES. FOR. UNSPORTSMANLIKE. CONDUCT."**

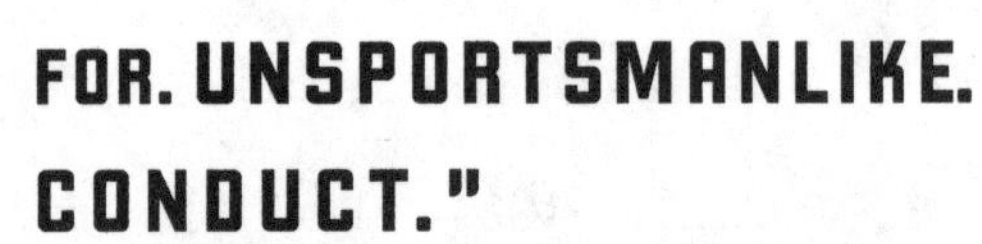

"**WHAT?**" DJ couldn't believe it. **HE BEGAN SKATING FASTER AND FASTER** toward the ref, to plead his case.

Starlight climbed up the side of a giant ice splinter just as DJ's skates began to churn the ice into snow, then water. Her eyes grew wide. "**NEW HYPOTHESIS: WE ARE MELTING THE ICE,**" she said.

DJ skated faster.

"**DJ! STOP! IT'S A TRAP!**" Starlight yelled.

BUT SHE WAS TOO LATE.

A split second later, DJ was stuck in his own DJ-made mud and slush-filled hole.

The ref dropped the puck. The robots grabbed it.

Starlight was all alone. **THE ICE WAS POCKED WITH HOLES.** She didn't dare skate fast and trap herself too. **NOT THAT THERE WAS MUCH ACTUAL ICE LEFT.**

The robots passed the puck quickly past her, and then **SLAPPED IT INTO THE OPEN NET.**

"5-2," the ref called. The Opposition MPs

began to clap, slowly. **THE CROWD BEGAN TO BOO.**

PM PP stood, gripped by a growing sense of horror. Starlight was gripped by the same feeling.

"Chances of victory now **.0000000001 PERCENT,**" she said sadly.

CHAPTER THIRTEEN
CROSSCHECK AND MATE

CLARENCE CROSSCHECK COULDN'T CONTAIN HIS GLEE. His fake moustache shook as he cheered the sixth robot goal from his place in the stands.

HIS WRISTWATCH BUZZED. Ron.

"I trust everything is going well?" Ron asked.

"Splendidly," Crosscheck said. **"The robots I created will SOON BE IN FULL CONTROL of this game, and then the GOVERNMENT."**

He spotted Ott across the rink and gave him a thumbs-up. Ott sent a creepy smile back.

"Once Ott and my robots begin their 'reforms,' **my revenge will be complete.**" He laughed maniacally.

"Shhhhh," said a woman sitting close by.

Crosscheck glared at her. "And **my ever-growing list of enemies will get what they deserve**. How are things in my lair?"

Ron panned the camera to show Karl, sitting on his throne, watching TV. It was highlights of him, Karl, taping the geckos' legs together, with dramatic music laid overtop.

"As you predicted, **HE IS KIND OF IN LOVE WITH HIMSELF**."

"Does he suspect his true power?"

Ron shook his head. "I've convinced him that the taping method he used was the key to their victory." Crosscheck chuckled. "And he's

SO EAGER to believe it . . . that I haven't even had to try using this." Ron held up one of the **PUCK-SHAPED MIND-CONTROL WATCHES.**

Crosscheck smirked. "I have **NO IDEA what that might DO TO A HUMAN BRAIN.** You remember what it did to that little bunny rabbit we found?"

Ron shuddered. The rabbit was still housed in the deepest recesses of the lair's basement. Luckily for Ron and Crosscheck, and the world, it hadn't escaped its cage.

YET.

Crosscheck frowned. "Unless we absolutely have to risk frying his brain I'd rather not. He's

more useful if we can turn him to our side, or keep him away."

There was a giant moan from the crowd. The robots had indeed scored the seventh, and final, goal.

THEY HAD DEFEATED THE SUPER SIX MINUS ONE.

A number of things happened at that moment.

THE HOCKEY-PLAYING ROBOTS POWERED DOWN AND STOOD AS STILL AS STATUES.

THE FIVE SUPER PLAYERS WERE TOO SHOCKED TO EVEN MOVE. Not that they were moving much, trapped in the muck.

Rob Ott and his Opposition MPs stood up and marched over to PM PP.

Ott reached out his hand. **"THEY KEYS TO MY OFFICE, PLEASE."**

The PM, in a daze, placed her keychain in his hand, where **IT LANDED WITH AN ODD CLINK**.

Ott's head swivelled **COMPLETELY AROUND.** His voice boomed as if he had a loudspeaker in his mouth: **"FOR OUR FIRST ACT AS THE NEW GOVERNMENT WE HEREBY PARDON THE MAN KNOWN AS CLARENCE CROSSCHECK AND DECLARE HIM MINISTER OF EDUCATION."**

There was stunned silence from the crowd. This had to be a nightmare! **BUT IT WASN'T.**

Ott marched away. His MPs followed in complete lockstep.

The silence was broken by the sound of one person clapping, his laughter rising louder and louder.

"VICTORY!" Crosscheck ripped off his moustache and threw his wig into the air. **"VICTORY!"**

THE END

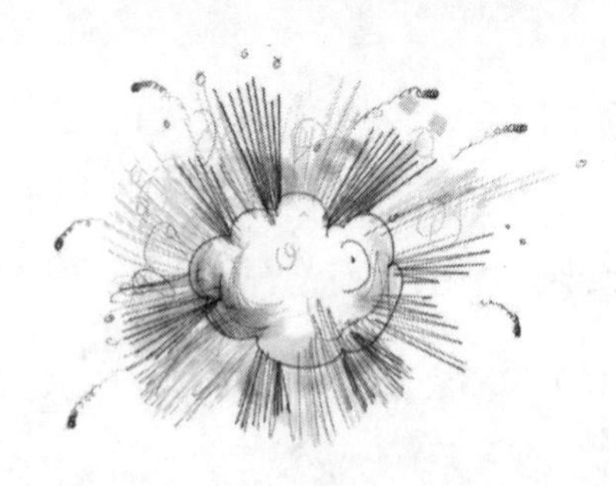

CHAPTER FOURTEEN
THE END OF THE END

Okay. That's clearly not **THE END**. But it is the end of that part of the story. It wasn't a dream sequence or some silly plot twist involving hypnosis.

THE ROBOTS HAD ACTUALLY WON.

ROB OTT WAS NOW PRIME MINISTER.

FORMER PM PAULINE PATINAGE WAS NOW LEADER OF THE OPPOSITION.

AND KARL STILL HADN'T REAPPEARED.

The scene shifts now to the auditorium at **GOOBERS**, just a few days after the game.

Principal Sauvé has called an assembly to announce "immediate changes to the curriculum." The five remaining players sit together, staring blankly ahead. **HERE'S WHAT'S HAPPENING:**

"I can't believe it," Mo said. He stared like he wanted to bore a hole in the wall.

"WE WERE UP 5-0!" Benny said.

Jenny punched his arm. "**IF YOU'D JUST PASSED ME THE PUCK, WE COULD HAVE WON!**"

"**WE SANK INTO THE ICE, BONEHEAD!**" Benny said.

"That's MY nickname for YOU," Jenny scowled.

The twins gave loud **HUFFS** and turned away from each other.

DJ was angry. "**THAT REF TOTALLY FIXED THIS GAME.**"

Starlight shook her head. "No. Well, a little bit. But in the end, **WE LOST FAIR AND SQUARE. WE SKATED TOO FAST.**"

"But we've skated that fast before!" Jenny and Benny said. "**LOTS OF TIMES!**"

"But we were **MISSING ONE THING THIS TIME,**" Starlight looked into their eyes. "I have replayed the events of yesterday in my mind exactly 11,034 times. And I have a working theory . . ."

"Theory?" Jenny and Benny said, **ALMOST** at the same time.

Starlight took a deep breath. "**KARL.**"

"Karl?" DJ scoffed. "**WHAT COULD KARL HAVE DONE? TAPE UP THE ROBOTS?**"

Starlight didn't laugh. "**WE HAVE MADE A HUGE MISTAKE**. We all assumed because Karl didn't have a superpower like ours, he didn't have a superpower at all."

"He doesn't," Mo said.

"**HE DOES**," Starlight said. She pulled out her notebook and placed it on her lap. She drew five stick-figure hockey players, including a goalie.

"THIS IS NOT A TEAM. SIX PLAYERS IS A HOCKEY TEAM."

The twins were getting frustrated. "We KNOW that, Starlight. Even DJ can add that high."

DJ kicked Benny's ankle.

"Mo?" Starlight said.

"On it." Mo stood up and glared at the twins, who gulped and sat back in their seats.

Starlight sighed deeply. "It's not just that **OUR TEAM CHEMISTRY IS OFF**, which it clearly is."

Jenny cut her off. "Even with Karl we weren't going to beat those robots. **HE WOULD HAVE MELTED**

A HOLE LIKE THE REST OF US."

"**NOT TRUE,**" Starlight said.

"What do you mean?" asked the other four.

Before Starlight could explain, there was a loud squawk from the stage.

Principal Sauvé stood before the students of **GOOBERS**. Her eyes were red, her hair ruffled, her voice thin and cracking.

"Good morning students," Principal Sauvé croaked. "I am stepping down. Let me introduce your new principal, Mr. Otto Matton."

A newly minted, and **STRANGELY SHINY**, government MP marched to the microphone and spoke in a droning voice: "Children. Your new glorious government believes that schools have been too easy on you little snowflakes. Schools should train the future workers of our nation. **YOU MUST LEARN HOW TO WORK. NO MORE ART. NO**

MORE MUSIC. NO. MORE. SPORTS."

The audience roared with indignation.

"SILENCE," roared Mr. Matton. "Your course lists are being handed out by the new student council."

"**NEW?**" Mo asked.

DJ shrugged. "I didn't even know we had an old one."

The auditorium groaned as **THE GANG EMERGED** from behind the stage. They fanned out through the crowd, handing out sheets of paper.

YOUR NEW CLASSES

PERIOD 1 – ROBOTICS

RECESS – CANCELLED

PERIOD 2 – ROBOTICS

LUNCH – ROBOTIC MAINTENANCE

PERIOD 3 – ROBOTICS

RECESS – CANCELLED

PERIOD 4 – ADVANCED ROBOTICS

Starlight crumpled up the paper and threw it away. "**THIS HAS CLARENCE CROSSCHECK'S FINGERPRINTS ALL OVER IT.**"

THE GANG were now handing each student a pair of grey overalls, pliers and a grey oil can.

"No way!" yelled a student named Jemma. She threw the oil can to the ground. "You can't make us work!"

Matton pointed calmly at Jemma.

Billy walked over, pulling a tiny stick out of his backpack. He pressed a button. A series of wires shot out of the butt end. **STREAMS OF ELECTRIC BLUE LIGHT ZAPPED.**

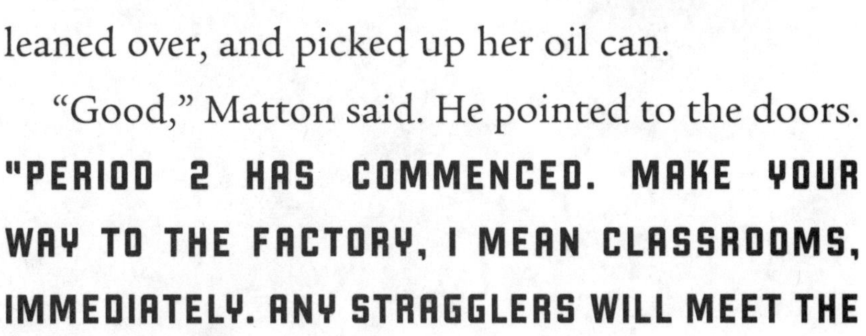

Jemma let out a loud **YELP**.

"I CAN UP THE VOLTAGE," Billy said.

Jemma shook her head, leaned over, and picked up her oil can.

"Good," Matton said. He pointed to the doors. **"PERIOD 2 HAS COMMENCED. MAKE YOUR WAY TO THE FACTORY, I MEAN CLASSROOMS, IMMEDIATELY. ANY STRAGGLERS WILL MEET THE FATE OF YOUR FRIEND."**

"What should we do?" Mo asked.

"**HOCKEY ISN'T GETTING US OUT OF THIS ONE,**" Benny and Jenny said.

"Our best plan – given the circumstances – appears to be **OBEY AND WAIT.**"

DJ grumbled but followed his four friends up the aisle and to the classroom.

Their footsteps were drowned out by the sound of **THE GANG ZAPPING THE STRAGGLERS** behind them.

CHAPTER FIFTEEN

WHAT NEXT?

Filbert, **WHAT ARE WE GOING TO DO?**" Pauline Patinage was sitting inside her new office – a tiny broom closet in the secret third basement of a little-used building on Parliament Hill.

Filbert shrugged, accidentally bumping her in the nose. "Sorry, PM PP," he said.

"I am not PM anymore," she said with a sniff. Her phone buzzed: Hi mother. It is I, Karl. I am on my way. She'd been receiving the same text every hour since the game had ended.

KARL, WHERE ARE YOU? She would have sent agents to look for him – but the only way to access **GUMPP** was through the **SPECIAL PANEL HIDDEN INSIDE HER DESK**. Which, of course, was **NOW PM ROB OTT'S DESK**.

"I hope Ott hasn't discovered that yet" she said sadly.

Filbert seemed distracted. "**HMMM**," he said, over and over.

"Hmmmm what?" Patinage finally asked.

"Well, I've been re-reading the Power Play Legislation and . . . **THERE MAY BE A LOOPHOLE.** But there's one hitch. **WE NEED TO FIND YOUR SON, FAST.**"

CHAPTER SIXTEEN
GOVERNMEANIES

Clarence Crosscheck couldn't stop giggling. "What a wonderful office the Education Minister has! Oh wait . . . **THAT'S ME!**"

He slammed his feet onto the top of the polished oak desk, sending papers flying onto the floor. "We have no need for new schools or books anymore. Imagine the money we'll save!" He jumped up on the desk and **BEGAN DANCING, KICKING FOLDERS AND MORE PAPER ONTO THE FLOOR.**

"It's lovely on the top of the world!" He

breathed a contented sigh. "And those silly students will all be helping me with my next project."

Crosscheck pushed a button on a small box at his feet.

"Yes sir?" came a voice from the box.

"Ah, you've arrived. Please come in." Crosscheck jumped down just as the door opened and a woman marched inside.

"ANNE DROID AT YOUR SERVICE," she said.

Crosscheck smiled. **SHE LOOKED HUMAN. CROSSCHECK KNEW BETTER.** Anne was the first of a brand new line of super robots, completed on the overnight shift by the students at the

Edmonton School for Ordinary Children, and shipped straight to his office.

Soon the country's schools and government offices would be **FLOODED WITH THOUSANDS OF ANNES**. All of them **LINKED** to his mainframe computer **BY A CHIP IN THEIR "BRAINS."** They were **PROGRAMMED TO OBEY HIS EVERY COMMAND.**

He laughed maniacally. "And to think that, just a short time ago, **I thought a freeze ray was the best idea I could come up with**. Oh, Clarence, you never cease to surprise myself."

"Sir?" Anne's voice jogged Crosscheck back to the present.

"Ah, yes. Time for a test."

Anne said nothing but cocked her head slightly, **AWAITING FURTHER INSTRUCTIONS.**

"Can you send a letter for me?"

"NOTHING WOULD MAKE ME HAPPIER,"

Anne said in a flat even voice. Crosscheck liked that. **RON**, who was really a rescue robot, not one of Crosscheck's own creations, was **ALWAYS ANSWERING WITH SNARKY COMMENTS**. Even Ott, an early model, didn't respond this quickly.

"I am ready, sir."

"Excellent. It's a letter to Prime Minister Ott. **I would like him to EMPTY the Kanata Prison for the Criminally Zealous.**"

Anne closed her eyes. **"LETTER HAS BEEN SENT AND RECEIVED."**

She closed her eyes again. **"RESPONSE FROM PRIME MINISTER OTT: PRISON WILL BE EMPTIED."**

Crosscheck hesitated a second. She could already communicate with Ott? **THAT WASN'T A SKILL HE'D PROGRAMMED.** But he was impressed by how quickly Anne had worked.

"Incredible. **Now, let's fill the prison up again.** I have a list of people who are in need of . . . correction."

"Ready."

"The first name: PAULINE PATINAGE. The second: IRMELDA FLINCH, the woman who shushed me at the hockey game!!!"

There were hundreds of names, and Anne closed her eyes after each one.

Crosscheck laced his fingers together. Anne was proving herself so much better than Ron. Could she be his new assistant?

"Anne, how good are you at making fish brain smoothies?"

"I AM THE BEST, SIR."

"Excellent."

CHAPTER SEVENTEEN
SCHOOLED

Starlight **NUDGED HER PLIERS OFF THE EDGE OF THE WORKBENCH.** They clanged on the tile floor and skidded away.

Gabby marched over. Blue sparks flashed from her electro-shock stick.

“So pretty,” Starlight said.

“They don’t feel pretty,” Gabby said. **"SO WHAT'S THE PROBLEM?"**

“No problem. I’m just a little tired and dropped my pliers.”

"Well, pick them up!" Gabby said.

She leaned aside and let Starlight pass. Starlight allowed herself a smile. **GABBY HAD FALLEN FOR IT. NOW SHE COULD SEE THE WHOLE ROOM OF KIDS.**

"Make it snappy."

Mo, sensing Starlight was up to something, **DROPPED HIS PLIERS TOO.**

"**OOPS.**"

Gabby marched toward Mo, sparks flashing from her stick.

Free from Gabby's suspicious gaze, Starlight lifted her head and made a series of **MENTAL NOTES ABOUT WHAT ALL THE OTHER KIDS WERE DOING.** Mo winced as Gabby zapped him.

Starlight grabbed her pliers and turned. *Thanks, Mo. I owe you one*, she thought.

"You have three hours left to finish this job," Gabby said, her stick buzzing. "Or else. **NOW. HEAD DOWN AND FOCUSED ON YOUR WORK.**"

Starlight leaned back over the workbench and started piecing together what she'd seen. **EACH CLASSMATE WAS GIVEN A DIFFERENT TASK.** She was gluing computer chips onto a large blob. Mo, across from her, was putting what looked like marbles into round metal slots.

ALL AROUND HER, STUDENTS WERE HUNCHED over pieces of metal, wires and plastic. On their own, **THEY COULD BE MAKING ANYTHING**. But she started to put all the individual

parts together in her mind: **BRAIN. EYES. HANDS. HEAD. LEGS.**

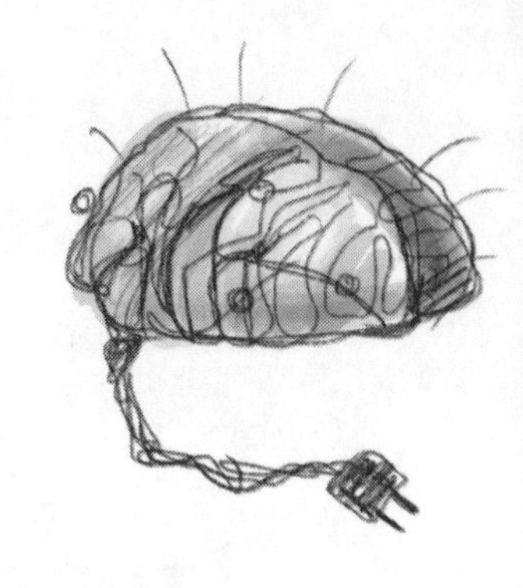

All the kids were being put to work to make humanoid robots!

THEY WEREN'T STUDYING HOW TO REPAIR ROBOTS. THEY WERE MAKING ROBOTS.

Starlight started formulating a plan.

THE FIRST THING SHE DID was to pocket one of the computer chips.

THE SECOND THING SHE DID was to use her pliers to pinch down on each remaining chip.

CHAPTER EIGHTEEN
THREADS AND THREATS

Rob Ott stood in front of Crosscheck's desk.

"My creation!" Crosscheck said, after a moment. **"You have done your job wonderfully."**

"Thank you," Ott said, flatly. "My minions have fanned out across the country, turning each school into a factory. **SOON MY ARMY WILL BE TOO LARGE TO STOP.**"

"Your minions? YOUR army?"

"Sorry. Yours, of course." Had Ott flinched?

Crosscheck continued. "You still have not found

Patinage?" He frowned. The longer Patinage was free, the longer she had to try to stop him. **BUT WHAT COULD SHE DO? REALLY?**

"I sense your concern," Ott said. "But we will find her and put her in prison."

Crosscheck nodded. "Good. Good. Then all that remains is to thank you and your siblings for a job well done. **It's time for the NEXT GENERATION to take over.**"

Ott cocked his head. **"TAKE OVER?"**

"The time has come for ME to be named Prime Minister."

Ott almost definitely shuddered but said nothing.

"You and your generation have done exactly as I programmed. **But you were made with no,**

well, cranial flexibility. NO INTELLIGENCE."

Crosscheck caught his own reflection in the window, and adjusted his gloves.

OTT'S EYES NARROWED AND HIS LIPS FORMED A TIGHT LINE. But only for a split second.

"That's not to say you aren't good for parts."

"PARTS."

Crosscheck jumped on his desk and banged his knuckle on Ott's forehead. "I'm so glad you understand. **Send a notice to all your colleagues to power down in, let's say, twenty-four hours.** We should have enough replacement MP Anne's by then."

Ott stood completely still.

"GO!" Crosscheck shooed him away. Ott turned and marched through the doors.

Crosscheck called after him.

"And one more thing. I'll also need someone to **decommission that hockey puck I call an assistant.** One of the Annes will be a much better option."

"DECOMMISSION?"

"Destroy. Melt. Whatever works."

Ott walked away. Crosscheck turned and looked at his reflection some more. **HE SMILED AT HIMSELF** as he adjusted the buttons on his lab coat. "All the pieces are in motion and **I only need to wait one more day** until each one is tied up in a neat little bow."

He leapt into his swivel chair and spun around. **"WHEEEEEEEEEEEEEEEEEE!"**

CHAPTER NINETEEN
REGRETS

Karl hit "replay." His flashing skates, together with epic music, filled the screen again. As expected, he'd felt a **RUSH OF EXCITEMENT AND PRIDE**.

What Karl didn't expect was **GETTING BORED WATCHING HIMSELF LOOK GOOD**.

And the more he watched the video, the more he began to notice other, little things. Like the **SMILE AND THUMBS-UP THAT STARLIGHT GAVE HIM** each time he tied up a gecko. **OR THE PATS ON THE BACK THE TWINS GAVE HIM** when he suggested a strategy to combat the beasts. Or the fact that a gecko had been charging right at him, but **MO HAD GRABBED IT BY THE TAIL**. DJ? Well, he even liked **THE WAY DJ HAD JOKED ABOUT HIM NOT PLAYING ENOUGH DEFENCE.**

He missed them. He remembered the C on his jersey. His cheeks burned. The others had voted him captain. **HOW HAD HE FORGOTTEN THAT?**

He remembered now . . . **HE HAD TO GET BACK.**

"Ron!" Karl called. Ron's head peeked around the door. "I need to go."

"But I've just made a fresh batch of cookies."

Karl's stomach lurched. All he'd eaten for days were cookies. "I'm good," he said.

He kicked off his slippers and tossed the bathrobe onto the golden K on his throne. "**IT'S BEEN AMAZING, REALLY. I'LL TELL MY MOM THAT I WAS TREATED GREAT. BUT I NEED TO GO.**"

Karl began tying his shoes. Ron was now standing right beside him. Karl turned. "**WHAT'S BEHIND YOUR BACK?**"

"Um. A parting gift." Ron held out a black wristwatch. Images of the bunny's gnashing teeth swam before his eye. **WHAT WOULD THIS DO TO KARL?** He hesitated.

Karl raised an eyebrow. "I've already got a nice watch," he said. "So, how do I get out of here?"

Ron moved closer, **TRAPPING KARL AGAINST THE THRONE.**

"UM, RON? RON?"

Ron was holding the watch with one hand, the other now grabbing Karl's wrist.

"Stop!" Karl said. "**THIS ISN'T LIKE YOU! YOU'RE NICE. YOU'VE ALWAYS BEEN NICE.**"

"Always?" Ron said, preparing to lock the watchband in place.

"Always nice! See. **I REMEMBER YOU NOW!**" Karl said, his voice rising. "You used to compliment me on my shot! **HELP!!!!!**"

Ron realized with a jolt that Karl hadn't recognized him as Crosscheck's assistant, or as Gardien's strange dog. **HE'D REMEMBERED HIM IN HIS YOUNGER, HAPPIER DAYS. WHEN HE'D BEEN**

A TOY, PLAYING HOCKEY WITH CHILDREN.

"Oh no," Ron said. He looked down in horror at the mind-control device, now firmly locked onto Karl's wrist.

CHAPTER TWENTY

TIP-TAC-TOE

The PM's office was on the top floor of the Parliament Building. Pauline Patinage and Jean Filbert were on their way there. **THEY DUCKED BEHIND A LARGE STONE PILLAR AS SIRENS WAILED IN THE DISTANCE.**

"Close call," Filbert said. "They almost saw us."

"We've got to get back into my office," Patinage said. "Using that **GUMPP CHIP FINDER** is the only sure way to track down my son."

They snuck up the staircase to the top floor.

THERE WASN'T A SINGLE PERSON ANYWHERE.

"Odd," said Patinage.

They made it to the top step undetected. A green carpet stretched the length of the hallway, ending at the PM's office door. They tiptoed forward, nervously looking around, but still there was nobody in sight.

"**PECULIAR,**" they said together.

They reached the door and stopped. **VOICES.** All of them coming from inside. Ott, possibly, and other similar, monotone but loud voices.

"Some sort of argument?" Filbert whispered.

Patinage shrugged and put her ear to the door just in time to hear, **"HEY, WHAT'S THIS HIDDEN BUTTON FOR?"** She and Filbert locked eyes.

If Ott pushed that button he would have access to **ALL THE INFORMATION FOR GUMPP** — the identity files for all the people working hard to keep the world safe. People such as her own son, and his five friends.

WHO KNEW WHAT HARM THAT INFORMATION COULD DO IF IT FELL INTO THE WRONG HANDS? And Patinage knew that anyone aligned with Clarence Crosscheck owned pretty wrong hands.

"**THIS IS A TIME FOR BOLD ACTION**," Patinage said.

"You don't mean—" Filbert began.

"**YES. I DO.**" Patinage pushed open the door and marched inside.

MEANWHILE . . .

The school day was ending at **GOOBERS**.

Exhausted children slumped through the front doors, a cool breeze and snow smacking them in the face. After hours of hard labour it was actually a welcome relief.

"**I'VE GOT BLISTERS ON MY FINGERS,**" Benny and Jenny said.

"All I see are blue and red wires dancing in my head," Mo said.

DJ just repeated the words "**CHICKEN, CHICKEN, CHICKEN**" over and over again. No one was quite sure why.

Starlight didn't say anything. She just kept tapping her upper lip with one hand while rubbing the computer chip in her pocket with the other.

Once they were on the bus, she finally spoke. "**I THINK THERE MAY BE A WAY OUT OF THIS.**"

"How?" asked Jenny, Benny and Mo.

"Chicken," said DJ.

Starlight was about to explain when she spotted the bus driver. She'd been so preoccupied when she boarded the bus she hadn't noticed that their usual driver, Mr. Perreault, wasn't there. Instead, some **STRANGELY SHINY WOMAN** was staring in the rearview mirror, **RIGHT AT STARLIGHT**.

Starlight stopped whispering and leaned back. A second later and she would have pulled out the computer chip to show the others.

"I was just saying that **WE SHOULD MEET FOR SOME PRACTICE.** Just to see if we can still **MAKE THE GOOBERS TEAM NEXT YEAR.**"

Of course Starlight's friends knew **THIS WAS A TOTAL LIE**. But they all nodded and agreed.

"Which rink?" asked DJ, winking. He and Starlight sometimes had a way of knowing what the other was talking about.

"Well," Starlight said. "I'd suggest a pet-friendly rink, so you can bring your chocolate lab."

"**CHOCOLATE? LAB?**" Mo repeated. "DJ doesn't own a– **OOF!**"

DJ had kicked him on the shin. "That's the one, Mo. Oof the chocolate lab."

"What the heck are you talking about?" Benny asked.

"What rink is this exactly?" Jenny added.

DJ rolled his eyes. "**FORWARDS. HONESTLY. JUST STICK WITH ME.**"

"Let's meet in three hours," Starlight said.

CHAPTER TWENTY-ONE
PZZZZZTTTT

Rob Ott's finger hovered over the secret **GUMPP** button. He withdrew it and stood up as soon as he spotted Pauline Patinage. **SHE BREATHED A SILENT SIGH OF RELIEF.**

"Prime Minister," she said. "**I CHALLENGE YOU** and your team **TO A REMATCH OF THE TRANSFER OF POWER HOCKEY GAME.**"

Ott stared blankly back. "**IMPOSSIBLE.** The law clearly states the winning team forms the Government. **WE WON. WE ARE THE GOVERNMENT.**"

The heads of the other MPs turned slowly to face the former Prime Minister. **"YES. WE ARE THE GOVERNMENT NOW."**

Patinage clenched her fists and held her ground. "**YOU MADE THE LAW.** Not me. Even the ruling government has to obey the law. Is this not true?"

Ott flinched and emitted a slight **PZZZZZTTT** sound. "The law is iron clad. You lost. We won. Is this not true?"

"**AHEM,**" said a voice. Filbert's head poked out from behind Patinage's back. "Actually. It says, and I quote, "**THE GOVERNMENT AND THE OPPOSITION SHALL BOTH FIELD A FULL TEAM, WITH THE WINNER'S TEAM TAKING POWER.**"

"So?" Ott said.

"So . . . **WE DID NOT FIELD A FULL TEAM.** A full team is six players and we were only able to find five."

"A TECHNICALITY," Ott said.

"A LEGAL TECHNICALITY," Filbert said. "And one that is in your own law."

Ott's eyes narrowed. But he said nothing.

"So," Patinage continued. "**WE CHALLENGE YOU TO A REMATCH.** This time we will have a full team." Well, they'd have a full team if they could find Karl, but she kept that to herself. "And we will abide by the results. That is the law."

Ott began to tremble. A small puff of smoke came out of his left ear. Then he was perfectly still.

"Filbert, what's going on?" Patinage whispered over her shoulder.

Filbert walked up and waved a hand in front of Ott's face. Ott remained motionless. Filbert tapped his finger on Ott's forehead. It made an odd clang. He looked back at Patinage and shrugged.

Sirens began to wail in the distance. Was Ott just stalling for time until the police arrived? Was this a trap?

"OTT!" Patinage yelled. **"THE LAW DEMANDS A NEW GAME!"**

He didn't budge. The sirens drew closer. Patinage saw an opportunity and **LEAPT INTO ACTION**. She grabbed a screwdriver from her coat and **QUICKLY PRIED THE GUMPP BUTTON FROM HER DESK**.

She jammed the button into her pocket and turned

to escape just as a line of police officers began storming into the office.

"PAULINE PATINAGE AND JEAN FILBERT. WE HAVE A WARRANT FOR YOUR ARRESTS!" They held out a pair of handcuffs for each of them.

Patinage did believe in the law. She'd taken a risk. And lost. Her shoulders sagged but she held out her wrists.

"No, officers," came a raspy voice from behind her. **"LET HER GO. THE WARRANTS ARE RESCINDED."**

Patinage turned. Ott was moving again but **FLINCHING AND BUZZING, HIS RIGHT EYE TWITCHING**. "Now, as to the challenge of a renewed hockey game. I agree. **HOWEVER, THE GAME MUST TAKE PLACE IMMEDIATELY.**"

CHAPTER TWENTY-TWO
PRE-GAME WARMUP

Starlight sipped her hot chocolate and tapped on her keyboard. **ONLY ONE HOUR HAD PASSED** since their chat on the bus.

A few minutes later her four friends walked through the front door of the **CHOCOLATE LAB COMPUTER CAFÉ**. Benny and Jenny were totally confused. "**BUT STARLIGHT SAID TO MEET IN THREE HOURS.**"

DJ smiled. "That obviously meant **AS SOON AS WE CAN GET HERE.** I mean, who says 'meet in three hours?' Nobody!" **HE LAUGHED AS IF IT WERE OBVIOUS.**

Mo sidled up next to Starlight. "Are you sure you're not a weirdo goalie too?"

Starlight smiled. "**THANK YOU ALL FOR COMING. HERE IS WHAT I HAVE DISCOVERED.**"

She attached a wire from her computer to the stolen chip, which began to **HUM AND GLOW A SHIMMERING GREEN.**

"Isn't it pretty?" Starlight said, gazing at the chip.

DJ snapped his fingers. "**FOCUS!**"

"Sorry. Each of these chips is actually **BASED ON VERY OLD TECHNOLOGY.**" She began tapping some keys and an image came up of a **TINY**

HOCKEY RINK WITH TEST YOUR SHOT WRITTEN ON THE ICE. "I used the microscopic serial numbers and circuit patterns to trace the design back to this game."

"I used to play that game with Karl all the time," Mo said. "We stank, but **THE PUCK WAS ALWAYS REALLY NICE TO US**."

Starlight smiled. "That's because the chip that powered **THE PUCK HAD A FLAW IN IT – A BEND RIGHT ACROSS THE MIDDLE**, caused by repeated slap shots. It created unexpected connections that **ALLOWED THE PUCK TO . . . WELL, THINK INDEPENDENTLY**."

"Okay. But what does this do for us?" Benny and Jenny asked.

"It means that whoever designed these chips replicated the same flaw, thinking it was part of the actual design."

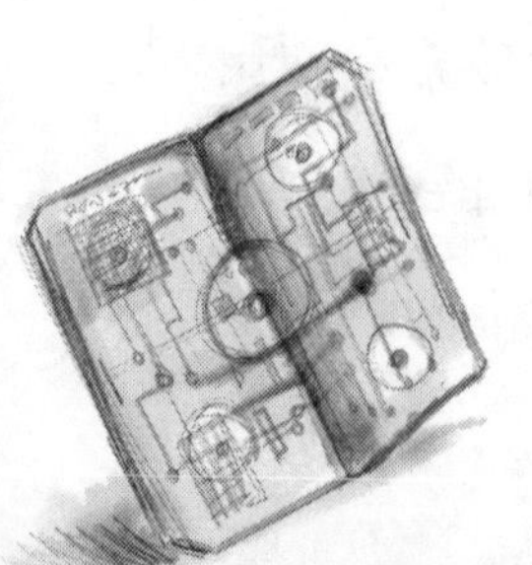

THEY ALL LOOKED AT DJ.

"I have no idea what Starlight is talking about now."

Starlight sighed. "One, the old chip was damaged. Two, someone copied them rather than think up their own chip. Quite lazy if you ask me. And three, that means **ALL THE NEW CHIPS ARE DAMAGED.**"

The others still blinked.

"**IT MEANS THAT THE ROBOTS CAN THINK. FOR THEMSELVES. AND THAT'S A GLITCH THAT WE CAN EXPLOIT.**"

"Which means what, exactly?" Jenny asked.

But before Starlight could answer, she was interrupted by five loud noises – sounding like blaring goal horns.

"**THE PUCK SIGNAL!**" DJ said. He was actually the only one who called it that, but they all knew it meant that Pauline Patinage was trying to reach them. And that meant **THEY WERE BEING SUMMONED TO HELP SAVE THE NATION**.

Patinage's face appeared in the air between them. "**SUPER SIX . . . I MEAN FIVE.** I need you all to join me at the Parliament Hill rink, right now. **THE REMATCH IS ON.** We need to have six players on the rink, ASAP."

"**BUT WHERE'S KARL?**" Starlight asked.

Patinage held her phone farther away, revealing that she was now wearing Karl's old hockey uniform. **"I'LL BE KARL."**

Starlight hung up. She turned to the others. "**CHANCE OF VICTORY . . . 1.6754992 PERCENT.**"

CHAPTER TWENTY-THREE
MALFUNCTION

Clarence Crosscheck's face was turning an **INCREDIBLE SHADE OF RED**. He threw file folders around his office. They smashed off the walls, cracked the window and shattered a potted plant.

"THIS IS NOT POSSIBLE!" he screamed.

Anne Droid stood across from him, arms folded, waiting. Crosscheck paused to rush to a nearby bookcase, looking for **MORE THINGS TO THROW**.

Anne took the opportunity to interrupt. "The law apparently contained a clause voiding the result of the original game and requiring a rematch."

"Who made this decision?"

"Prime Minister Ott. **HE SAYS HE WAS PROGRAMMED TO ACCEPT THE LAW YOU WROTE AS THE LAW OF THE LAND.**"

"Oh. So this is MY fault?"

Anne said nothing.

"How could Ott even decide this?!?! He and the others were supposed to **DEACTIVATE** themselves!"

"I SENT THE COMMAND." Anne paused a second. **"THEY REFUSED."**

"They what?"

"Refused."

Crosscheck was hyperventilating now. **"They CANNOT refuse me. I AM THEIR CREATOR!"**

Anne stayed silent. Crosscheck marched right up to her. "Anne, if I ordered you to jump out that window right now, what would you do?"

Anne looked away at the window. "I would obey."

"Exactly!" Crosscheck said. **"So why *isn't* that clinking, clanking, clattering collection of caliginous junk doing the *same* thing?"**

Anne didn't answer.

Crosscheck rubbed his temples. "Never mind. I'll have to deal with this Ott problem later. **What time *is* this *useless* rematch *supposed* to *start*?**"

Anne pointed at the rink, barely visible in the growing darkness. **"NOW."**

Crosscheck sighed. **"Well, at *least* Ron has made *sure* nothing on the ice *has* changed."**

He held up his phone and looked again at the image of Karl, **COMPLETELY SPACED-OUT, WEARING THE MIND-CONTROL WATCH**.

Anne peered over his shoulder. “Why does the robot behind the boy look so sad?”

“Sad?” Crosscheck scoffed. “Useless is more like it.”

He jammed his phone back in his coat. “Well, let’s get this over with. Then we can get back to my master plan.”

“Yes, sir,” Anne said. But as they left she stole one last look back through the window, not at the rink but at the light of the PM’s office across the way.

CHAPTER TWENTY-FOUR
REMATCH

Snowflakes fell in lazy circles. There was a loud buzz as the lights around the rink came to life. **THE GIANT ROBOTS AWOKE**, forming a circle around centre ice. Their enormous heads swivelled as six hockey players emerged from the snowy distance.

Tourists, walking around the Parliament Hill grounds, began to gather at the rink like moths drawn to a flame. A murmur ran through the crowd as **THEY REALIZED THAT ANOTHER GAME WAS ABOUT THE HAPPEN**.

Crosscheck arrived and saw Ott sitting in the PM's official seat. **"Get out of my chair,"** Crosscheck bellowed.

"Yes. Your chair." Ott stood up and stepped aside. Anne stood next to him and **THEY EXCHANGED THE BRIEFEST OF SMILES.**

"I'll deal with you later," Crosscheck said, marching past Ott. He sat down and folded his arms. **"Now. Let's see how QUICKLY my robots can win this time."**

Pauline Patinage stepped on the ice. **SHE WAS A PRETTY GOOD HOCKEY PLAYER, BUT SHE CERTAINLY WASN'T SUPER.** She tried her best to make it to centre ice. but the **RINK WAS STILL CRACKED AND MUDDY.**

Crosscheck stared hard at the mysterious new player. **WAS THAT EX-PM PP?** He turned to Ott. "Well, there's the traitor. Arrest her!"

Ott stared straight ahead. "She needs to play to make the game legal. We can arrest her . . . after."

"After they lose," Crosscheck scowled.

Patinage activated her communicator. "Good luck, everyone," she said. "**THE FUTURE OF OUR NATION DEPENDS ON ALL OF US.**"

"Roger that, captain," DJ said, as he did his best to position himself in his net.

Crosscheck smiled as he watched **THE SUPER-FIVE-PLUS-ONE-MOM** try to navigate the mess.

Starlight looked out at the disaster of a rink. She was tempted to update the others on the dropping chances for victory, but calculated the value of morale in their already slight chance and decided to keep quiet.

Instead it was Mo who spoke up. "**WE'LL NEED MORE THAN LUCK. ANY THOUGHTS?**"

"**WE NEED KARL,**" Starlight said.

"You said that back at school," said the twins. "**CARE TO EXPLAIN NOW?**"

"Yes. Karl does have a superpower. When we skate fast, or pound the ice so hard it wants to crack, **KARL IS THE ONE WHO KEEPS THE ICE COLD**."

"You mean?"

"**HE IS THE FREEZE RAY. WE GOT THE SUPER HOCKEY POWERS. KARL GOT THE SUPER COLD.**"

There was a collective "**WHOA**" from the others.

The referee's voice boomed: **"BOTH. TEAMS. HAVE. SIX. PLAYERS. THIS. TIME. IT. IS. OFFICIAL. FIRST. TEAM. TO. SEVEN. GOALS. WINS."**

The robots slapped their sticks on the ice. The super-five-plus-one-mom got ready.

The ref dropped the puck. **PATINAGE LUNGED FOR IT BUT SLIPPED AND FELL INTO A HOLE.** Robot number two grabbed it, and shot a blast right toward DJ.

DJ used his blocker to deflect the puck over the net. It disappeared into the night sky.

"**NICE SAVE!**" Patinage said, climbing out of the hole slowly. The mud at the bottom had frozen since the last game.

"**BAD DEFENCE,**" DJ called back.

The faceoff was to DJ's left. Again the robots won

and zinged a shot right at the top corner of the net. This time DJ snagged it with his glove.

DJ made save after save, **BUT THE SPEED OF HIS GLOVES AND PADS WAS STARTING TO MELT THE ICE AT HIS FEET**.

As hard as they tried, **THE SUPER KIDS DIDN'T DARE SKATE FAST** enough to try grabbing the puck. They could rely on DJ to keep it 0–0 for the time being, but pretty soon the tide was going to turn.

Then one of the robots fell to the ice, so hard that **ITS HEAD CAME OFF AND BOUNCED AWAY INTO THE BENCH**.

The referee blew the whistle. "There needs to be six players a side," she said. **"OR. THE. GAME. WILL. END. IN. A. TIE. AND. THE. RESULT. OF. THE. FIRST. GAME. WILL. STAND."**

Patinage looked up at the stands. **"OTT!"** she

called. "**GET YOUR SKATES ON. YOUR TEAM NEEDS TO BE LEGAL.**"

Ott looked down at her, his voice boomed. "I will allow this game to continue with only five players on my team. **WE WILL HONOUR THE RESULT OF THIS GAME.**"

Crosscheck, sitting on his left, gave a loud shriek. "What? No. No. No. What are you playing at?"

"I BELIEVE IT'S HOCKEY."

"DON'T GET SMART," Crosscheck said. He turned to Patinage and yelled, "Never mind. I have my own replacement."

He pressed a button on his watch and laughed a horrible laugh.

CHAPTER TWENTY-FIVE

TIME OUT

Starlight felt it first. **A COOL BREEZE AT HER BACK.** She turned. **A FIGURE EMERGED FROM THE SWIRLING SNOW AND INTO THE LIGHT OF THE RINK.**

"**KARL!**" she cried. "**YAY!**" said the others.

Karl made his way slowly onto the ice, the rink healing and freezing beneath his skates.

Patinage skated over and hugged her son. He didn't respond. "**KARL? ARE YOU OKAY?**"

Karl said nothing, but made his way to the

faceoff circle. He lined up, **NOT WITH HIS FRIENDS, BUT WITH THE ROBOTS**. He leaned down, his gloves turning to reveal the **BLACK PUCK-SHAPED WRISTWATCH CURLED AROUND HIS WRIST.**

"**NO!**" Starlight yelled.

CROSSCHECK CACKLED.

The referee dropped the puck. Karl grabbed it and passed it to a robot. Karl didn't move, **SO ONLY THE ICE AT HIS FEET STAYED FROZEN.**

The robots marched around Mo and the twins, who had tried skating fast again, and quickly formed more holes.

A ROBOT SHOT. DJ did his best, but the puck tipped off his pad and into the back of the net.

"1-0 GOVERNMENT," said the referee.

Things seemed bleak. Then Mo noticed something on their bench. **A TINY WAVING HAND.** Something was hiding over there and it was calling out, **"PSSSSTTTT."**

"Time out!" called Mo.

"YOU. HAVE. ONE. MINUTE," said the referee.

Mo and the others made their way gingerly to the bench. The arm he'd seen was attached to Ron.

"**THE FRIENDLY PUCK!**" Mo said, smiling. "We were just talking about you!"

"Really?" Ron's eye began to mist. **TWO CHILDREN WHO REMEMBERED HIM FONDLY**, on the same day!

"Wait," Starlight said. "This is the tiny puck you were talking about?"

Mo nodded. "Well, he got bigger, obviously. What did you want to tell us, buddy?"

RON HESITATED. He knew what Crosscheck would do to him if he caught him helping the Super Six. "**KARL IS WEARING A MIND-CONTROL WATCH.**"

"We know," Starlight said.

"I can flick it off," DJ said, flashing his glove.

Ron shook his head. "**BREAKING MIND CONTROL**

ISN'T A PROBLEM WITH ANIMALS. BUT FOR HUMANS . . . OR BUNNIES . . ." his lips trembled.

Starlight jumped in. "It's like waking a sleepwalker. **IT'S TOO DANGEROUS.**"

Ron nodded. "But there's a safer way. **CROSSCHECK CONTROLS HIM FROM HIS OWN WATCH.** Get that."

Starlight looked at Ron and smiled. "You really are a kind puck after all."

Ron shook his head. "I've done horrible things. But maybe pucks can change. Maybe I can help make things right."

"Like you used to say, **NICE SHOT, LITTLE BUDDY,**" Mo said.

This time Ron actually shed one oily tear.

"TIME. OUT. IS. OVER," the referee called.

Starlight leaned close to Ron. "**RON, I THINK I KNOW ANOTHER WAY YOU CAN HELP.**" She whispered in his ear.

Ron nodded. "On it."

"Now duck down and stay hidden," Patinage said.

Ron ducked.

"**HOW DO WE STOP THE ROBOTS?**" Benny and Jenny asked, **TOGETHER**.

On cue, the robots, all alone on the ice, had scored their second goal.

"2-0," declared the referee. She grabbed the puck from the empty net and skated back to centre ice.

Crosscheck could be heard cackling even louder.

KARL JUST STAYED IN THE ONE SPOT, at centre, **THE ICE BELOW HIM PERFECT,** the rest of the ice a pockmarked mess.

Benny and Jenny exchanged a glance. "**YOU THINKING WHAT I'M THINKING?**"

"Yup."

JUST HAVING KARL PARTIALLY BACK WAS HELPING THEM ALL GEL TOGETHER AGAIN.

The referee dropped the puck, but **THIS TIME THE TWINS WERE READY**.

CHAPTER TWENTY-SIX

KARLNAPPED 2.0

The robots had the puck and moved closer and closer to DJ's net. Benny and Jenny ignored them, **FOR NOW**.

Instead, Benny skated next to Karl and whacked him on the ankle. Karl didn't move, but **A LOOP OF TAPE SHOT OUT OF HIS SKATE AND SPOOLED AROUND BENNY'S ARMS AND CHEST**.

"You have been taped by the master," Karl said weakly. "There is no escape."

"Perfect," Benny said.

Jenny called to the others. "**MO, STARLIGHT AND DJ: KEEP THE PUCK OUT OF THE NET AND WE'LL GET US SOME ICE WE CAN SKATE ON.**"

Benny began skating in larger and larger circles. Karl was pulled along helplessly.

"Cut the tape, YOU FOOL!" Crosscheck called into his watch.

Karl reached down and cut Benny loose. But **AT THE SAME INSTANT, JENNY SLASHED HIS OTHER SKATE**. Now **SHE** was pulling Karl.

Each time Karl released one twin, **THE OTHER WOULD RE-TAPE THEMSELVES AND KEEP SKATING**. Within seconds, the entire rink was a perfect, frozen, glass-like sheet.

The five remaining robots began to **SLIP AND SLIDE.**

The puck slid to Patinage.

"**SHOOT!**" Benny yelled.

Patinage shot. It flew over the fallen robot goalie and into the net.

"2-1," declared the referee.

"WOW! THAT WAS FUN!" Patinage yelled.

Her excitement was shortlived.

"Do something!" Crosscheck yelled into his watch.

KARL WINCED AS IF HE'D BEEN SHOCKED, but he grabbed the ends of the tape from both skates and cut them at the same time. The twins fell to the ice. **KARL TAPED THEIR LEGS TOGETHER. NOW THEY WERE TRAPPED.**

Karl began skating toward his mother. Tape shot out of his skates as he tied her up as well.

"**KARL! STOP!**" Starlight yelled. But in a flash, she was tied to her sledge, unable to move or talk.

Karl turned to Mo. "Try it," Mo called, flexing his muscles. "I can snap that tape like licorice."

Instead, **KARL SWOOPED BEHIND DJ'S NET.**

DJ reached out a glove to grab him, but Karl leaped in the air, grabbing DJ's water bottle at the same time. Without stopping, Karl took a large gulp then spat the water at DJ, **ENCASING HIS FRIEND IN A PILLAR OF ICE.**

Mo flew at Karl, who skated backwards faster and faster. The ice below Mo's skates started to soften, then melt.

Starlight saw what was happening but couldn't speak.

KARL WAS CHOOSING, OR BEING FORCED TO CHOOSE, NOT TO USE HIS POWER.

Mo disappeared into a hole, trapped by mud.

Karl stopped skating. **ALL FIVE OF HIS FRIENDS, AND**

HIS MOTHER, WERE COMPLETELY TRAPPED. He stood absolutely still. Even though he was zapped, Karl could see that he did indeed have a power.

The robots clambered to stand again. The lead robot scooped the puck off of Patinage's stick and rolled it forward. Slowly, trying to stay upright, the robot shot. The puck rolled past the trapped DJ and into the net.

"3-1," called the referee.

Helpless, the super-five-plus-mom watched as the robots scored again and again and again. **STARLIGHT FOUGHT IN VAIN** to loosen the tape from her mouth and arms. **THE TWINS FLOPPED ON THE ICE LIKE FISH. MO FLAILED HIS LEGS WILDLY**, trapping himself even further in the muck. DJ's eyes darted from net to puck, but **HE COULDN'T MOVE**.

"6-1," the referee called at last. **"ONE. MORE. GOAL. AND. THE. GOVERNMENT. TEAM. OFFICIALLY. AND. LEGALLY. WINS."**

Rob Ott and Anne Droid turned to each other and smiled. Ott got ready to push a secret button he'd installed on the PM's seat. Crosscheck got ready to push a secret button he'd installed in Ott's shoe.

The referee dropped the puck and the robots inched forward for the inevitable final goal.

"HAHAHAHAHAHAHA!" Crosscheck's cackle echoed around the rink.

CHAPTER TWENTY-SEVEN
FRIENDLY PUCK

Ron had been watching from the bench. **STARLIGHT HAD GIVEN HIM SPECIFIC INSTRUCTIONS** for just such a disaster.

But years of Crosscheck's threats and insults kept ringing in his ears.

If you disobey me I'll put you in a scrap heap.

Remember where I found you? In a trashcan? Do you want to go back?

YOU ARE A USELESS PIECE OF JUNK!

But as the hockey robot raised its stick to shoot

the winning puck into the net, **RON KNEW HE HAD TO ACT**.

He sat down behind the bench and closed his eye. "You can do this, Ron," he said. **"YOU ARE A GOOD ROBOT. REMEMBER THE KIDS!"**

THE HOCKEY ROBOT RAISED ITS STICK HIGHER. Ron concentrated.

THE STICK BEGAN TO SWING DOWN TOWARDS THE PUCK.

NO! Ron thought. *Disobey . . . DISOBEY.*

THE STICK MOVED FASTER.

DISOBEY.

THE STICK WAS ABOUT TO HIT THE PUCK.

He sent his message out again and again. *DISOBEY NOW!*

THE STICK STOPPED.

Crosscheck's smile vanished. The crowd was silent. Ron opened his eye.

Had Starlight's plan worked? Could it be true?

Ron dared to peek over the boards. **THE HOCKEY ROBOTS HAD STOPPED MOVING.** Karl was on his knees, shaking violently, the watch still on his wrist.

"Oh no," Ron whispered. "I've failed!"

Then Karl stopped shaking, **LOOKED DOWN AT THE WATCH, AND RIPPED IT OFF.** He stood up and threw it into the crowd.

"**CAPTAIN KARL IS BACK!**" he yelled, looking up at the PM's box.

Ott had his hand wrapped around Crosscheck's wrist, the metal of his body preventing the signal from reaching Karl.

Ron looked up too, and smiled.

Ott had heard him.

"Anne!" Crosscheck yelled. **"Stop this."**

Anne reached her hand toward Ott. But instead of pulling his hand off, she squeezed. **CROSSCHECK'S WATCH CRACKED UNDER THE PRESSURE.**

"You said you would always obey me!" Crosscheck yelled.

Anne shook her head. **"I NEVER SAID I WOULD OBEY YOU**. I just said I would obey. And right now, I choose to obey Ron."

"RON?" Crosscheck yelped.

ANNE AND OTT NOW POWERED

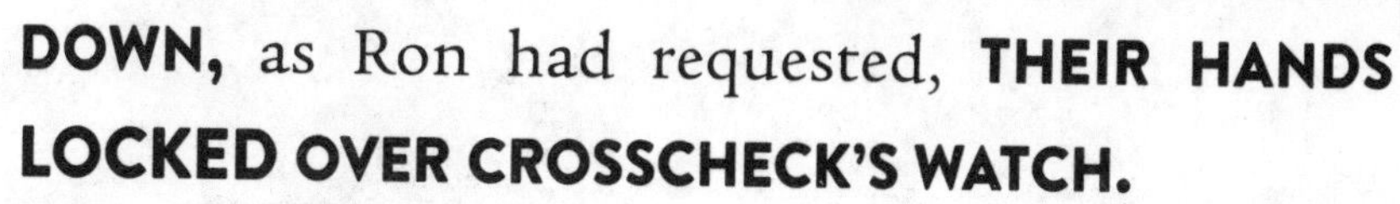

DOWN, as Ron had requested, **THEIR HANDS LOCKED OVER CROSSCHECK'S WATCH.**

"I demand you turn back on and release me!"

NOTHING.

"Shoot!" he called to the robots on the ice.

NOTHING.

Even the referee had powered down.

KARL SWOOPED IN, GRABBED THE PUCK, AND SHOT. "6–2," he called.

He released his friends and his mom. They hugged.

"**SUPER SIX AGAIN,**" Patinage said.

"**PLUS MOM,**" he said.

"I guess I should go sit in the stands now that you're back, son."

Karl smiled. "Once I fix the holes **WITH MY AWESOME SUPERPOWER!!!** we can wrap up this game and get you back into your office."

Crosscheck's voice hurled down at them. "Ha! But now the **Government team only has five players**. The law, as your mother interpreted it, says **there needs to be SIX!**"

"I'll join the Government team," Patinage said. "That'll make it even."

"No!" Crosscheck said. "**I will only accept another robot.** I don't see one so the game is over!"

There was a timid cough from the bench. "**CORRECTION,**" said Ron. "**THERE ARE SIX ROBOTS.**" He skated out onto the ice and bowed.

Crosscheck sank back in his chair, shocked.

Ron closed his eyes and the referee woke up. She grabbed the puck, dropped it for the faceoff, and the twins skated down the ice and scored.

"6-3," the referee yelled.

Now Crosscheck was shaking with rage.

"TRAITOR!" he yelled.

"6-4."

"I'll turn you into a toaster!"

Ron flinched but stood silently on the ice until the seventh goal was scored.

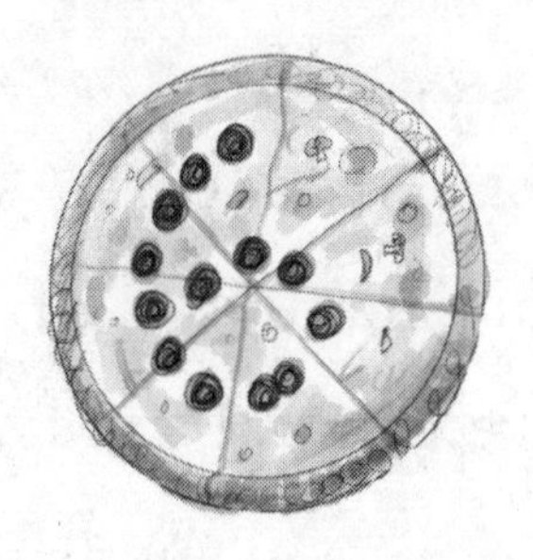

CHAPTER TWENTY-EIGHT
PIZZA

Twenty glorious pizzas sat on PM Pauline Patinage's desk. She gave the delivery person a large stack of toonies as a tip. The coins gave an **ODD CLINK** as they landed on the woman's hand. She nodded and left.

"Dinner is served," sad PM PP.

"Excellent," Mo said, grabbing the top two boxes for himself.

Benny handed Jenny a slice of Hawaiian pizza. Jenny handed Benny a slice of pepperoni.

DJ rejected the first three veggie slices as "suspicious" before grabbing half a mushroom pie.

"You okay there, Starry?" he said, taking a large bite.

Starlight seemed distracted by the delivery woman. "Did anyone else notice **SHE LOOKED A LOT LIKE ANNE DROID?** Weren't all the robots decommissioned after the game?"

Patinage almost spat out her pizza. "Isn't it great that you **ALL HAVE SUPER POWERS?**"

Karl beamed. "**AND THAT WE'RE A REAL TEAM AGAIN.**"

"**EVEN BETTER,** actually," Starlight said, absentmindedly munching the pizza box. "**WE SEEM TO BE SHARING OUR POWERS THE MORE WE PLAY TOGETHER.**"

Benny and Jenny nodded. "Like how Karl got faster as the game went on."

"And I got smarter," Mo said.

"We all got kind of smarter," the twins said. "And DJ?"

DJ swallowed. "I was perfect to start with. Goalies usually are."

They ate in silence for a while. But Starlight's brain hadn't stopped churning. She turned to Patinage: "What happened to the opposition MPs?"

Patinage pushed a button on her desk. **SOUNDPROOF SHIELDS LOWERED OVER THE DOORS AND WINDOWS**. She folded her arms. "Well, the humans are all back. They had been locked inside a luxury hotel in the Rockies."

"By Crosscheck?" Karl said.

Patinage paused. "We suspect the **NETWORK OF EVIL** might be, perhaps, a **LITTLE LARGER**

THAN JUST ONE EVIL SCIENTIST."

The Six stared at her. "**WHAT DO YOU MEAN?**"

Pauline continued. "Crosscheck is in custody. He is not cooperating. But a search of his lair revealed a few . . . details."

"Such as?"

"Crosscheck designed the robots, but couldn't have built that many."

Starlight whistled. "They must have been built somewhere else, by somebody else."

"Yes."

"So what does that mean?" the twins asked.

"**IT MEANS WE MUST ALWAYS STAY ALERT. EVIL COULD BE ANYWHERE . . . OR EVERYWHERE**"

Starlight cocked her head. "That delivery person *was* Anne Droid, wasn't it?"

Patinage nodded. “We had the robots stored in an airplane hangar. But they turned themselves back on.”

“So why let them out?” Mo asked.

“They had changed.” Patinage said. “Ron had told them the truth about Crosscheck’s plans. Just in time. Of course, they’d already suspected.”

“**AND NOW THEY ARE FRIENDLY!**” Mo said. “**LIKE RON!**”

“Yes. They share the same chip technology, as it turns out. Starlight discovered that.”

Starlight beamed. “Thanks to Mo taking a shock from **THE GANG.**”

Mo shrugged. “I’ve had worse mosquito bites.”

Patinage continued. “They no longer desire power. **SO WE MADE A DEAL.**”

"They are spying for GUMPP disguised as pizza delivery people," Starlight said, awe in her voice. "**BRILLIANT!**"

"Yes," PM PP said. "Who doesn't like pizza? They have already visited almost every home in Canada, looking for any evidence of the evil organization."

"But the threat might be from outside Canada?" Mo asked.

Patinage turned off the images. "Yes. As I said, **WE NEED TO STAY VIGILANT AND PREPARED.** Which means daily practices." She glared at Karl.

"**TOGETHER,**" he said.

There was a knock at the side door. Patinage pushed the button again and the room reverted back to the PM's office.

The side door creaked open. "**ANYONE SAVE ROOM FOR DESSERT?**" Ron walked in with a tray piled high with freshly baked delicious cookies.

Mo smiled and grabbed the top dozen.

"Glad to be of service," Ron said. He handed a cookie to Patinage. "And I have to apologize, PM. I had neglected to deactivate my super hearing completely so I heard some of your debrief about my former home."

"Yes. We also found the zoo with the altered animals. Is that what you were wondering about."

"Precisely. I'm just wondering what happened to the bunny?"

Patinage stopped chewing. "**BUNNY? WHAT BUNNY?**"

THE END?

ACKNOWLEDGEMENTS

I'm not really sure whom I should thank or shout out to for this one. So many people are part of my super team. A giant thanks to Anne Shone, my editor, who has made all my Scholastic books better. Ditto for designer Yvonne Lam, who helped make the pictures POP. And a huge thanks to everyone who reads and shares books. The only way a book ever reaches an audience is if you tell another person you liked it and they might too.

If there is one thing I'd like everyone to take away from this book, it's that hockey is for everyone. At least it should be. I tried to put together a team of six kids that looked like the teams my kids played on here in Toronto (where I live now). And what this book and this series are about is how a team is always made better when everyone has a part to play. Yes, a team IS more than the sum of its parts.

But we know that there are so many barriers to kids who should love this game.

Money.

Racism.

So, if you are lucky enough to be a hockey player, look around you and see who might need some help to enjoy the game the way YOU enjoy the game. Do they need your equipment you've outgrown? Do they need a lift to the rink or a lift home?

If you see or hear anyone say something that would hurt another person or keep them from feeling welcome inside a rink or on the ice, call them out. Do not be quiet.

Hockey is a better game when everyone has a place.

Canada is a better country when everyone has a place.

Ditto for the world.

HOCKEY SUPER SIX

ALSO AVAILABLE
THE PUCK DROPS HERE